"Well, hell. You really did a number on yourself."

T.J.'s gaze had dropped to the middle of her chest. Glancing down, Jordan saw a mottled bruise already forming on the hand gripping the towel.

"It's nothing. I just hit my hand on the counter when I went down."

He crossed the room in two strides. "Better let me take a look at that."

"Hey! Do you mind? I'm naked here."

"Yeah, I noticed," was T.J.'s response. "Give me your hand, Red."

And release her death grip on the towel? Jordan didn't think so. "What are you going to do?" she jeered. "Kiss the boo-boo and make it better?"

His grin slipped out then. The same grin that used to give her quivers. "The NYPD first responder's medical training didn't include kissing as a treatment option.

"But I'm certainly willing to give it a shot."

Dear Reader,

I've visited Hawaii many times but was struck all over again by its beauty when my husband and I cruised the islands a few months ago. Jagged mountains, lush vegetation, steep ravines—nothing like all that wild splendor to fire a writer's imagination and get her thinking about perfect spots for clandestine operations and/or buried bodies!

Then there's the romance of the islands. How could anyone *not* fall in love on a spun-sugar beach kissed by tropical breezes and soft, shimmering waves? Sigh... So naturally I had to set Book #1 in the continuation of my CODE NAME: DANGER series in beautiful Hawaii. Hope you enjoy the adventures of T. J. Scott and Jordan Colby, aka Diamond, as much as I did.

And be sure to watch for Book #2, coming from Silhouette Desire in May 2006. Set along the coast of Baja, Mexico, *Devlin and the Deep Blue Sea* involves a tough, sexy undercover agent, a chopper pilot working the offshore oil rigs and a particularly smarmy shark.

All my best,

Merline Lovelace

MERLINE LOVELACE

DIAMONDS CAN BE DEADLY

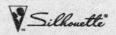

INTIMATE MOMENTS™

Published by Silhouette Books

America's Publisher of Contemporary Romance

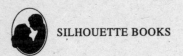 SILHOUETTE BOOKS

ISBN 0-373-27481-5

DIAMONDS CAN BE DEADLY

Copyright © 2006 by Merline Lovelace

Printed in U.S.A.

Books by Merline Lovelace

MERLINE LOVELACE

spent twenty-three years in the U.S. Air Force, pulling tours in Vietnam, at the Pentagon and at bases all over the world. When she hung up her uniform, she decided to try her hand at writing. She's since had more than fifty novels published, with over seven million copies of her work in print. Watch for *Devlin and the Deep Blue Sea,* the next book in the CODE NAME: DANGER series, coming in May from Silhouette Desire.

For my sweetie and that never-to-be-forgotten
evening on the balcony of the Sheraton Hawaii!

Prologue

*I*t was the kind of party only Georg Vostok could throw, a fifty-thousand-dollar-a-head gala to benefit victims of the devastating earthquake that had all but destroyed his native Chekistan. Vostok had skimmed the very top layers of Palm Beach's vacationing elite. Movie stars rubbed elbows with Armani-clad mafia. Politicians and poet laureates poured booze down their throats with equal enthusiasm. A sleek, well-known madame smiled seductively as she sized up potential clients. There was even a smattering of royalty.

The arrival of an elderly French duke barely stirred a ripple of interest, but the American-born wife of the sultan of D'han stopped all conversation

*dead when her bodyguards escorted her into the
soaring glass foyer of the Institute of Modern Art.
Blond and bronzed, the sultana had traded her burqa
for a strapless white evening gown that showed off
her slender curves and formed a perfect backdrop for
the Star of the East. The 900-carat oval emerald was
set in a plain gold bezel suspended from a gold chain.
Shooting sparks of green fire, it drew every eye at the
gala.*

*A smile rearranged the lines of Georg's dour,
craggy face. Thrusting his Baccarat champagne
flute at a waiter, he hurried forward to greet her.
"Barbara. You have come!"*

*The sultana brushed past her bodyguards, took
Vostok's outstretched hands and stooped for a kiss.
"For you, my darling Georg, anytime."*

*"No, no! For my beloved Chekistan." His smile
faded. "You cannot imagine the horror. I tell you,
Barbara, I have seen nothing like it. It haunts my
dreams, my every waking moment."*

*"We'll help, Georg. My husband has earmarked
fifty million for immediate aid, and we'll—"*

*She broke off, her delicate nose wrinkling. She
was too well mannered to mention the odd smell, but
her host had already picked up on it. Frowning,
Vostok sniffed the air.*

*"What is this stink? Excuse me, Barbara. I
must—"*

That's all he got out before he gave a small, in-

articulate grunt. His eyes rolling back in his head, he slumped to the floor.

"Sultana!"

The bodyguards shoved forward, but before they could reach their charge, her legs seemed to give out and she crumpled where she stood. The larger of the two men went down almost on top of her. The other dropped like a felled ox a few feet away.

An aged dowager in a collar of priceless pearls let out a shrill scream. Her thirty-something escort cursed. A tuxedo-clad waiter dropped a tray of champagne flutes and stumbled to his knees.

Five seconds later, the entire glittering throng lay sprawled across the black-and-white tiled floor.

Chapter 1

April was in full bloom in Washington, D.C. A gentle breeze rustled through branches budding with tender green. Forsythia flowered in great, showy bursts of yellow. Daffodils, tulips and crocuses sprang from pots and planters on almost every stoop, while tourists from around the world strolled the Tidal Basin under canopies of blooming cherry blossoms.

The graceful, Federal-style town house just off Massachusetts Avenue stood ready to greet the spring. Windows scrubbed clean of winter grime sparkled in the afternoon sunshine. The front door gleamed with a fresh coat of cinnabar paint. The discreet brass plaque set beside the door had been polished to a loving shine.

The plaque identified the town house as home to the offices of the president's Special Envoy. Most Washington insiders knew that the Special Envoy was one of those meaningless positions created several administrations ago to give a wealthy campaign contributor an important-sounding title and an office in the nation's capital.

Only a select few were aware that the Special Envoy's offices occupied just the first floor of the town house. Fewer still knew that the other floors served as the headquarters and home base of a covert government agency. An agency whose initials comprised the last letter of the Greek alphabet. An agency whose operatives were sent into the field only as a last resort, when all other government remedies had failed.

One of OMEGA's agents was preparing to go into the field now. The director had yanked her out of New York and was personally conducting her mission pre-brief.

A former operative himself, Nick Jensen was the owner of a string of outrageously high-priced watering holes for the rich and famous. His international contacts—and hefty contributions to several presidents' campaign chests—made the tall, tanned sophisticate a natural choice for Special Envoy. His years as a field operative gave him the experience and edge to take over as director of OMEGA.

Initially, Nick had chafed at being tied to a desk.

His subsequent marriage to Mackenzie Blair, OMEGA's chief technical adviser, had reconciled him—somewhat—to his current duties. He felt the weight of those responsibilities now as he clicked a remote and brought up a slide on the floor-to-ceiling screen dominating OMEGA's high-tech Control Center.

"This is the Star of the East."

Jordan Colby, code name Diamond, slid her half glasses to the tip of her aristocratic nose. A one-time model turned eyewear designer, she studied the oval-cut emerald with a coolly assessing eye.

"Quite a rock. I've read about it. Nine hundred-plus carats, isn't it?"

"Nine hundred and seven," Nick confirmed. "It was mined in Zambia in 1963 and purchased by the then sultan of D'han for a cool five million. The current sultan presented it to his bride as a wedding gift."

The next slide was a digitized security-camera shot of the sultana entering the Palm Beach soiree.

"I've read about her, too," Diamond commented. "She's come a long way since graduating from Yale."

"Where she happened to share a dorm room with the president's sister-in-law," Nick added dryly.

With a slither of silk crepe, Diamond uncrossed her legs and tipped her boss a droll look over the rim of her glasses. "Is that why OMEGA got handed this op? Silly me, I thought it had something to do with the millions of barrels of oil we import from D'han each year."

"Let's just say the president is extremely displeased that the wife of a friend and ally sucked in a lungful of benzilate gas at a charity event held on American soil and woke up twenty minutes later minus her wedding present."

"And that's the only item that was taken? The Star of the East?"

"The only item."

Shifting in his seat, Nick studied the operative he'd assigned this mission. Jordan still looked and carried herself like the model she'd once been. Long-legged, slender, she surveyed the world through gold-flecked amber eyes framed by a mane of shoulder-length auburn hair.

As Nick knew all too well, however, external appearances could be and often were deceiving. His gaze settled briefly on the logo embedded in one lens of the half glasses perched on the tip of her nose. That tiny diamond butterfly was more than a trademark. It represented the brutal cocoon the woman known to the world as Jordan Colby had emerged from.

The details were sketchy. Diamond never talked about her past. Only a few trusted insiders with access to her highly confidential background dossier knew she'd once laid into her stepfather with a tire iron and escaped into the icy night, a bruised and frightened fifteen-year-old.

The dossier included only vague references to where or how she'd lived until she burst into the limelight as a sultry-eyed runway model for a top New York designer some years later. After several seasons under the lights, she'd opted out of modeling to design high-end eyewear. Her jeweled sunshades and reading glasses now sold for more than three grand a pop.

Nick had recruited her to work for OMEGA. He'd trained her himself, knew her lethal skills. He also knew the stakes for this particular mission.

"We're talking more than oil and emeralds here, Diamond. We're talking a possible link to a man suspected of laundering billions in drug money."

Another click brought up a glossy PR photo of an internationally renowned psychotherapist and self-styled guru of Greene Tranquility, a multimillion-dollar industry that promoted the healing power of emeralds.

"Ahhh," Jordan murmured, studying the boyish face that smiled back at them from behind a lectern. "I should have guessed Bartholomew Greene would be involved in this. He has a thing for pretty stones the same color as his name."

"More than a thing. Greene tried to buy the Star on two separate occasions. He also tried to purchase the 600-carat Patricia Emerald, currently residing in the American Museum of Natural History in New York."

Nick zoomed in for a head-and-shoulders shot.

"According to what we've dug up so far, Greene was born Bartholomew Crynyk. He reportedly suffered from epileptic seizures as a boy. During one of the seizures, his grandmother draped a rough-cut Russian emerald around his neck. The fit subsided. Miraculously, he claims. He believes the gem's soothing qualities cured him and he became an instant convert. Eventually he even changed his name to reflect his absolute belief. He now preaches a combination of transpersonal meditation and stone therapy as a remedy for every illness."

Diamond's lip curled into the closest thing to a sneer her perfect features could achieve. She didn't comment, but Nick guessed what she was thinking. There were some sicknesses only a tire iron could cure.

"We theorize Greene's fixation with emeralds was what got him into the money-laundering business," he said. "Colombian mines produce the finest-quality emeralds in the world. Greene requires a steady supply of stones to sell to his millions of followers. The deals he's negotiated with sources in Colombia look legit on the surface, but…"

"But we both know nothing's legitimate in that corner of the world."

Frowning, Diamond hooked her reading glasses atop her head. The graphite frames caught her hair back in a tumble of red-gold.

"I take it you want me to infiltrate Greene's inner circle, sniff out his system for helping his pals in

Colombia convert their drug dollars to pesos and, oh by the way, retrieve the Star of the East."

"That about sums it up." Nick's tanned, handsome face creased into a frown. "You won't be the first undercover operative to attempt a penetration. DEA tried to insert an agent last year. According to our friends in the Department of Justice, he's dropped off the radar screen."

Diamond took the news with a nod. This wasn't her first op. She understood the risks.

"I see why you pulled me in for this mission. I have the perfect cover. I can approach Greene about a line of glasses for his thousands of disciples."

"With a butterfly logo."

One delicate brow arched. "Of course. But done in emeralds instead of diamonds."

"We've pulled together a detailed briefing on Greene's Tranquility Institute in Hawaii. Floor plans, security system, employees, a complete dossier on the master himself. I've got Claire Cantwell standing by to brief you on Greene's modus operandi. She'll act as your control for this op. Also, the wizards in the field dress and technology units have devised an interesting suite of accessories to outfit you for this mission."

"Oh, Lord!" Diamond couldn't quite suppress a groan. "The last time I went into the field, I carried enough electronics to launch the space shuttle. I hope your wife doesn't load me down like that on this op."

Nick merely smiled. Once chief of communications for OMEGA, Mackenzie now served as technical adviser to a loose conglomerate of governmental agencies that included OMEGA. To Mac's delight, her electronic toy box had expanded exponentially with her increased responsibilities. When it came to high-tech gadgetry, Nick's dark-haired, vivacious wife believed more was better and too much was best.

He left Diamond with instructions to check in with him when she'd completed her mission prep.

Jordan's mission preparation took the rest of the day. Her first session was with Claire Cantwell, code name Cyrene. A noted psychologist in her other life, the slender, delicate blonde had lost her husband in a bungled attempt to free the kidnapped oil executive years ago. She'd buried her grief behind a serene facade that disguised her absolute dedication to stamping out the kind of economic terrorism that had claimed her husband.

Drawing on her training and years of experience as a practicing psychologist, Claire gave a slide presentation attempting to explain Bartholomew Greene's healing methods.

"Transpersonal psychotherapy offers itself as an interface between traditional psychology and spiritual transcendence."

"Riiiight."

Cyrene accepted the underlying sarcasm in the

drawled comment with an unruffled smile. She and Jordan had worked together in the field. The two operatives respected each other's strengths. They also recognized their weaknesses. Claire's was a certain too-handsome Latin American by the name of Colonel Luis Esteban. Jordan's was her refusal to allow her past to intrude on her present. Sooner or later, Claire had suggested in her quiet way, Jordan would have to reconcile the two.

"The therapist supplements traditional techniques such as behavior modification or psychoanalysis with practices designed to elevate the patient to a higher level of awareness of self. The ultimate goal is a fusing of the physical and spiritual, thus providing a deeper, broader and more unified sense of identity."

Jordan forced herself to pay close attention as Claire presented a crash course in meditation therapies, alternative medicine and theories concerning the healing properties of gemstones. When Claire finished, she had to admit to more than a degree of skepticism.

"So you're telling me I'm going to find a bunch of middle-aged flower children chanting and rubbing colored stones when I get to Hawaii."

"Something like that." Claire clicked off her last slide and regarded Jordan thoughtfully. "You understand it isn't going to be easy getting close to Greene. His Tranquility Institute is supposedly open to anyone willing to fork out the ten grand required for a week-long session with the master, but we know his people screen every applicant closely."

"I'm not going in as an applicant. I'm going in as a designer of very exclusive, very expensive eyewear that will allow the man to gouge his followers even more."

"That's your entrée, of course. But don't underestimate Greene. He couldn't have gained such a large following without exercising considerable skill as a therapist. Or developing keen insights into people."

Jordan stiffened. "What are you saying? That I should pass myself off as a candidate for therapy?"

"What I'm saying," Claire replied quietly, "is that Greene isn't going to do business with anyone without without checking their background. He'll see the holes in yours and wonder about them."

"Let him wonder."

Jordan hated the ice that coated her voice. She'd trust Claire with her life. Yet she couldn't bring herself to talk about her past, even with this cool, composed friend. And she certainly wouldn't discuss them with a psychobabbler like Bartholomew Greene.

"Just be prepared," Cyrene advised calmly.

The warning lingered in Jordan's mind as she met with Mackenzie Blair and her electronic wizards. As always, Mac had come armed with a full bag of tricks.

"This is the latest in sniffers. We've souped it up a little for you."

Her eyes gleaming, the former naval officer palmed what looked like a compact, handheld CD player. It *was* a CD player, Jordan discovered when Mac grinned and depressed a button.

"You can listen to Travis Tritt while you search for listening devices, hidden cameras or electronic sensors. In receive mode, this little baby will pick up and interpret any and all electronic vibrations. In send mode, it could fuzz those signals temporarily or put them out of operation on a permanent basis."

After a few bars of "Too Far To Turn Around," Mac set aside the sniffer and briefed Jordan on an array of other equipment that included a thermal suit designed to contain body heat, thus defeating infrared sensors and night-vision goggles. She saved a pair of slender gold hoop earrings for last. One of the earrings was just what it looked like— a decorative piece of jewelry. The other was Jordan's primary means of communication while in the field.

"Just thumb the slight indentation at the back of the hoop," Mackenzie instructed. "You'll be able to receive and send clear voice-stream signals off a secure satellite. We'll monitor for transmissions around the clock."

Nodding, Jordan traded her diamond studs for the lightweight gold hoops. She was testing the astonishing clarity of the transmissions when word came that Lightning wanted to see her and Claire.

Mackenzie decided to accompany the two operatives downstairs to her husband's office. A specially shielded elevator zipped the three women to the first floor. The titanium doors wouldn't open unless the Special Envoy's executive assistant activated a silent release.

Trim, silver-haired Elizabeth Wells manned the ornate Louis XV executive assistant's desk. She'd worked for several of OMEGA's directors including Adam Ridgeway, his wife, Maggie Sinclair, and now Maggie's handpicked successor, Nick Jensen. Her cheerful efficiency was matched only by her skill with the .9mm Sig Sauer concealed in a special compartment in her desk drawer.

Jordan greeted the grandmotherly assistant with a smile. "Hi, Elizabeth. What's up?"

"I don't know, dear. Lightning just said he wanted to see you. Let me tell him the three of you are here."

Mackenzie winked at the two operatives. "That's Elizabeth's polite way of saying not even the Special Envoy's loving wife gets access to his office without clearance."

Her wicked grin said that restriction extended *only* to his office.

Once Elizabeth had cleared them, the three women entered the inner sanctum. It was furnished to suit the Special Envoy's exalted status. An acre or so of polished mahogany served as a conference table. His double pedestal desk was wide and long enough to serve as a landing pad for the space shuttle. Tall, wingback leather chairs stood in a window alcove, grouped around an antique map chest containing priceless charts Nick had collected over the years.

Rounding his desk, Lightning shared a quick smile with his wife. "Do you have Diamond all rigged out?"

"Right up to her ears."

"I'm good to go," Jordan confirmed, flicking back her hair to display the gold hoops. "Or I will be, once I work up designs for a whole new line of glasses, fire off a proposal and arrange an appointment to discuss the line with Greene in person."

"Yes, well, we've run into a slight complication." Nick smoothed a hand down his Italian-silk tie. "I had our folks run another screen of all guests and employees at Bartholomew Greene's Tranquility Institute. Seems he recently hired a new chief of security. TJ Scott."

Jordan's heart stopped, then restarted a second or two later with a painful kick.

Thomas Jackson Scott. The man she'd once tumbled so quickly, so *stupidly* in love with. The bastard who'd hurt her far worse than her heavy-handed stepfather ever had.

His face grave, Lightning gave her the option. "Do you still want to go in?"

"Oh, yeah." Jordan's lips curved in a feral smile. "No way I'd pass up a chance to nail a crooked faith healer *and* a dirty cop."

Chapter 2

"There's a Jordan Colby at the gates of the compound, boss. I have her on screen six."

TJ Scott's muscles went tight under the green-knit polo shirt that constituted his duty uniform these days. He'd spotted Jordan's name on the access list, knew she had an appointment with Bartholomew Greene this afternoon. He'd had plenty of time to prepare himself for this moment. Yet it took a conscious effort of will not to drop the report he was reviewing and whip around.

He forced himself to scrawl his initials on the report before he lifted his gaze to the bank of monitors that took up almost an entire wall of the Tranquility Institute's security operations center. The new, state-of-the-art digital cameras he'd had installed after his arrival a few weeks ago captured the driver who sat behind the wheel of the rented Mustang in excruciating detail.

She hadn't changed. Not outwardly. The hair only half confined by a designer silk scarf was the same shoulder-length waterfall of red. Those high cheekbones and full, sensual lips might have leaped right off one of the dozens of glossy magazine covers she'd graced over the years. She wore a minimum of jewelry, only gold hoops at her ears and designer sunglasses with the tiny diamond butterfly logo that had become her signature.

And there, just above the left eyebrow, was the small, leaf-shaped scar. The only flaw in an otherwise perfect face. She'd shrugged aside TJ's question about how she'd gotten it, giving only a vague reference to a childhood accident. He'd always thought it made her human.

It was one of his favorite spots to drop a kiss. Right up there with the slope of her breasts and the smooth curve at the base of her spine. The memory of her taste and scent drilled into him. For a moment, he could almost smell the unique blend of Chanel and warm, musky female that was burned into his senses.

Christ, he thought in disgust. All this time, and the woman could still put him in a sweat.

"She's on the access list," he growled to the on-duty security officer. "Run her through the drill."

Nodding, the officer keyed his mike. "May I see some identification, Ms. Colby?"

She fished a driver's license out of her wallet.

"Hold it up a little higher, please."

The camera captured the number and fed it to the institute's computers. They in turn would run it through a half-dozen databases, most of them legit.

"Thank you. Now remove your sunglasses."

"Excuse me?"

"For the security of our guests, we perform an iris scan of all personnel entering the institute's grounds. Please remove your sunglasses."

Frowning, she slid the glasses to the top of her head. The camera mounted at eye level whirred a few inches closer to capture an image of her left iris. A second later, it shot the right.

TJ had insisted on this very sophisticated, very expensive scanning system as one of his first upgrades to the institute's security. The iris was the most individually distinctive feature of the human body. No two persons had the same iris pattern, even identical twins. Cameras could scan that pattern in real time, unlike the minutes or hours or sometimes days required for DNA or fingerprint sampling and matching.

"Thank you, Ms. Colby. You may proceed to the main reception center. Just follow the signs to Kauna Cove. One of our staff will issue a welcome packet and show you to your bungalow."

* * *

Jordan dutifully followed the signs through acre after acre of gorgeously landscaped grounds. Graceful, swaying palms climbed to impossible heights. Hibiscus, sweet-smelling ginger and stately birds of paradise blossomed everywhere, adding a heavy fragrance to the salty tang of the sea.

Set on a bend of Kauai's rugged coast, the Tranquility Institute encompassed sweeping vistas of nature at its most elemental. Jagged volcanic peaks covered with dense vegetation stood like silent green sentinels against an achingly blue sky. Their steep slopes cut straight down to the waters they'd thrust out of so many millennia ago. Waves rolled in, foamed against the black volcanic rock at their base, and sent lacy spumes leaping high in the air.

The views were so incredible Jordan slowed at one turn to drink them in. Even as her soul responded to the raw, untamed beauty, her mind was imprinting the layout of the grounds, noting various facilities, and plotting escape routes.

There didn't appear to be many. The steep cliffs surrounding the institute dropped straight to the sea. Where not covered by vegetation, their slopes showed razor-edged creases of black volcanic rock, made even more slick and dangerous by the spume. The only descent was a set of wooden stairs that led to a small, protected beach fringed with palms.

On the landward side, the gate Jordan had driven through appeared to be the single egress point in the twelve-foot-high iron fence almost hidden by the lush tropical foliage. The fence was topped by pointed spikes that would be a bitch to scramble over.

Jordan eyed the iron barrier thoughtfully. She could go under it, of course. Or through it. She had a special pneumatic tool tucked at the bottom of her carryall that would pry the bars apart. She suspected, however, either of those alternatives would set off a half-dozen different alarms, silent and otherwise. TJ Scott was nothing if not thorough.

Her stomach twisting at the thought, she shoved the rented Mustang convertible into gear and followed the curving drive to the main reception center. The plantation-style building featured a high-pitched roof, fanciful white trim and a wraparound porch designed to protect the interior from Kauai's frequent showers. Thronelike rattan chairs invited guests to laze in the shade of the veranda, while swirling fans stirred the perfume of the orchids spilling from a series of hanging baskets.

Jordan parked beside a golf cart painted a deep emerald color with a green-and-white-striped awning. Skirting the cart, she started for the veranda. Only then did she spot the figure shaded by the deep overhang. He was leaning against a pillar, arms crossed, eyes shielded by mirrored sunglasses.

Waiting for her.

Despite being forewarned, despite the hours Jordan had spent steeling herself for this meeting, her heart started to pound. Sweat dampened her palms and the perfumed air she dragged into tight lungs was suddenly too sweet, too cloying.

She was damned if she'd let the bastard see his impact on her, though. Pretending a nonchalance she wasn't anywhere near feeling, she mounted the veranda steps.

"Aloha, Jordan."

She went still, knowing he would expect her to recognize the deep Bronx baritone. Turning, she slid her sunglasses to the end of her nose.

"Well, well," she drawled. "Look who's here...."

"Welcome to Hawaii."

He strolled over to where she stood and draped a lei of white orchids over her head. Somehow Jordan managed to resist the urge to rip off the garland, toss it onto the porch and grind the delicate blossoms under her heel. She didn't bother to disguise her scorn, however, as she let her gaze travel over his tanned face.

Every feature was seared in her memory. The strong, square jaw. The nose with the irregular bump on the bridge. The tobacco-brown hair cut military short. The mouth that had driven her so wild.

Infuriated by the memory, she aimed a pointed glance at the logo on his emerald green polo shirt and pretended ignorance of his position at the institute.

"So this is what happens to cops who go bad," she observed with a lift of her brow. "They wind up working as bellmen at tropical resorts for a living."

"It's worse than that," he drawled. "I'm in charge of security here. I don't even rake in any tips."

"I'm sure you'll find a way to skim off some cream."

He didn't rise to the bait, but Jordan spotted a small twitch at the side of his jaw. Deliberately, she slid the knife in deeper.

"Tell me, Scott. Does your present employer know the reason for your abrupt departure from the NYPD?"

"He does."

"And he trusts you with his security? Bartholomew Greene must be a forgiving man. Or very, very foolish."

Or so deeply involved in the same seamy underworld that had entangled TJ Scott, he'd jumped at the chance to bring the disgraced cop into his fold.

"Isn't Greene worried you'll betray his trust? The way you did your badge?"

"I didn't betray my badge, Red."

The pet name brought her chin up. She raked him with a withering look, not bothering to disguise her scorn.

"I suppose some people might not consider accepting bribes from petty criminals a betrayal. The squad from the anticorruption task force voiced another opinion when they kicked in your apartment door and found a suitcase stuffed with cash in your closet."

The shame of that night came rushing back. She and TJ had been asleep when a splintering crash

jerked them awake. He'd lunged for his service
pistol and rolled naked from the bed. Jordan had
dived for the neat little .38 she carried when not in
the field. She could still hear the shouts and
bellowed warnings, still remember the chaotic confusion of those first few seconds. Even now her
cheeks burned with fury when she recalled how two
members of the squad had stood watch while she
and TJ dragged on their clothes.

That scene had been bad enough. The worst came
a few moments later. To this day Jordan carried with
her the absolute mortification of discovering that a
highly trained and otherwise perceptive OMEGA
agent had fallen for a dirty cop. A cop who still
claimed he was set up.

"I said it then. I'll say it again. That wasn't my
suitcase."

The rough edge to his voice told Jordan he was
fighting for control. The knowledge gave her a
vicious sense of satisfaction.

"Tell it to the judge, Scott. Oh, wait! You already
did, didn't you?"

"And he dismissed the case against me."

"Because of a technicality," she shot back. "Some
low-level clerk at the NYPD put the wrong apartment number on the search warrant."

Fury bubbled to the surface, scorching away the
hurt. She snatched off her glasses and let him have
the full force of her contempt.

"It didn't matter what the witness said. That

whole chorus of pimps and street pushers who swore they paid you to stay off their backs. I would have believed you, TJ. I *did* believe you until the police report came back and confirmed your fingerprints were all over those bills."

She'd kicked herself over and over for missing the small signs that, in retrospect, were so damn obvious. The gold Rolex. The Italian loafers. The weekend at that ritzy Connecticut resort.

Her only excuse was that it had all happened so fast. They'd met at a charity event to benefit children of NYPD officers who'd died in the line of duty. The next afternoon they'd shared a blanket at an open-air concert in Central Park. The following Saturday they'd zipped up to Connecticut for the wildest, most heart-pounding forty-eight hours of Jordan's life.

She could almost—almost!—forgive herself for missing the signs that the cop with the linebacker's shoulders and sexy grin was on the take. What she couldn't excuse was how she'd fallen for the man so fast and so hard.

She knew better, dammit! All those years when she'd lived from hand to mouth, lying about her age, taking any job she could, she'd never let any male get close to her. The bone-deep wariness her stepfather had instilled with his fists had colored her every relationship with adult males. And despite the sultry image she projected on the runway, she'd never promised more than she intended to deliver. Until TJ.

Disgusted all over again at her acute lapse in

judgment, Jordan angled her chin. "We've had this conversation before. Several times. Is there any point to continuing it?"

He opened his mouth, bit back whatever he was going to say and shook his head. "I guess there isn't. See you around, Red."

"That's right," she muttered, her eyes on the broad shoulders covered in green-and-white jungle print. "You most certainly will."

TJ moved with the same lazy grace that had always characterized him. Even in those awful days after his arrest, his shoulders had stayed square and his long legs ate up the ground in an arrogant, self-confident stride.

Wrenching her gaze away, Jordan yanked open the door and approached the receptionist. Dark-haired, dark-eyed and lovely in a ruffled muumuu, the woman greeted her with a warm smile.

"Aloha. Welcome to the Tranquility Institute."

"Aloha. I'm Jordan Colby. I have a reservation."

"Oh, yes, Ms. Colby. I have your welcome package waiting for you."

Reaching under a counter made of a solid slab of gnarled wood, she produced a slim folder.

"This contains a map of the grounds and a schedule of daily activities. There's also a note from Mr. Greene's personal assistant, confirming your appointment with him later this afternoon."

"I don't see a key to my cottage," Jordan commented, shifting through the packet.

"You don't need a key. Entry to all facilities is by visual recognition. All you have to do is look into the blinking red light beside the door. Are your bags in your car?"

"Just a briefcase and carryall."

"If you'll give Danny your car keys, he'll fetch them and transport you to your bungalow."

Jordan eyed the map and saw her cottage was one of a half dozen scattered along the cliffs overlooking the Pacific. The route looked simple and uncomplicated.

"I'll drive myself."

"Oh, no, ma'am." Shaking her head, the receptionist signaled to a native Hawaiian the size and shape of a sumo wrestler. "We don't allow private vehicles beyond this point. To maintain tranquility, the guest cottages and activity center are also telephone and television free. We ask that you leave your cell phone here at the desk to avoid disturbing the other guests."

She smiled prettily, her teeth white against her skin.

"There's a communications room here in the reception center with TV, phone, fax and Internet services if you need to keep in touch with the outside world."

The tiny transmitter/receiver embedded in the gold earring would keep Jordan in touch with the outside world. She didn't really require her cell phone and wouldn't use it in any case to communicate with OMEGA, but decided to make the point that she hadn't come as a guest.

"I'm here to see Mr. Greene on business," she said firmly. "I need to retrieve messages and maintain contact with my employees. I won't carry my cell phone with me when I leave my cottage, but I will be using it and my laptop computer while I'm here."

The receptionist looked doubtful but was too well trained to argue with a guest.

"Very well. Danny, will you take Ms. Colby to her cottage, please?"

Big, bulky and exuberantly cheerful, Danny steered the golf cart along a path of crushed lava rock and pointed out the institute's facilities. All the buildings were constructed in the same turn-of-the-century territorial style as the reception center, with steep, hipped roofs, green shutters and wide verandas.

"That's the Lotus Spa," Danny said, indicating a structure surrounded by swaying royal palms. "The spa café serves light breakfasts and lunches. Carrot juice and macadamia-nut salads and stuff like that," he said with a shrug that suggested full-figured males like him needed heartier fare. "Regular meals are served from 6:00 a.m. to midnight at the Jade Buddha Restaurant. It's over there, beside the waterfall."

Jordan followed his pointing finger to a sparkling cascade that splashed downward from a bank of ferns into a three-tiered pool. At the upper lever was what appeared to be an elegant, open-air restaurant.

At the lower level, water escaped in another silvery stream and plunged a hundred feet straight down into the sea.

"Room service is available twenty-four hours a day," Danny assured her. "Best thing on the menu is the poke baked in seaweed."

"Po-keh. Got it."

"That's the Meditation Center." He hooked a thumb at a structure surrounded by flowering hibiscus. "Dr. Greene conducts all group sessions there. Private sessions are held either there or at his office."

"Which is where?"

"His office? It's in our corporate-headquarters building."

Jordan consulted the printed map and saw that the central headquarters was set apart from the rest of the resort, along with several smaller administrative buildings and quarters for the staff.

"I understand you have an appointment with Dr. Greene at four," Danny said as he pulled up at a cottage perched at the edge of the bluff. Rolling his bulk out of the golf cart, he retrieved her briefcase and bag. "I'll swing back by and pick you up a few minutes before four."

He stood aside for Jordan to activate the iris-recognition system. Stooping a little, she looked into the tiny camera eye mounted beside the door. A second eye, she noted, was positioned almost at waist level. For children, she surmised, or wheel-chair-bound guests.

"How do the maids get in to clean?" she asked when the door clicked open.

"They knock," Danny replied, following her inside, "and if they get no answer, security authorizes an override."

Jordan didn't particularly care for the fact that TJ Scott controlled access to her bungalow. She knew it was standard operating procedure. All hotels required room entry for maintenance, servicing and the safety of their guests in emergency situations. Still, she'd make sure to set a few intrusion-detection devices so she could ascertain *who* went in and out of her rooms.

"This is your sitting room," Danny said. "The bedroom and bathroom are through that louvered door."

Given the exorbitant fees guests paid to stay at the resort, Jordan had anticipated sybaritic luxury. These rooms lived up to her expectations and then some. Exquisite Oriental art hung on walls painted a delicate coral. The furniture was an eclectic mix of rattan and dark, heavy antiques. Floral prints in mint green and coral provided splashes of bright color, while plantation shutters, overhead fans and potted palms added a distinctly tropical flavor.

But it was the view that stopped Jordan in her tracks. The plantation shutters framing the east wall of the sitting room were folded back, so that the interior of the cottage seemed to flow out onto the covered lanai. Beyond the lanai was a stunning vista of jungle-covered peaks saw-toothing up from a turquoise sea. Transfixed, Jordan could only gape at what looked like a Hollywood creation of paradise.

"This cottage has the best view of Ma'aona," Danny commented as he deposited her briefcase on the sitting-room desk.

"Ma'aona?"

He directed her attention to a needle-sharp peak spearing high above the others.

"It's a holy mountain, sacred to ancient Hawaiians. They threw people who broke *tapu*—the old laws—from the top of Ma'aona onto the rocks below."

Tough bunch, the ancient Hawaiians.

"The burial site at the base of the mountain is off limits," Danny advised, "but you can drive up to the state park near the peak."

Jordan didn't figure she'd have much time for visiting ancient archeological sites. With another glance at the jagged peak, she dug her wallet out of her shoulder bag.

Her driver refused the bill with a merry smile. "There's no tipping anywhere on the grounds of the institute. It's our pleasure to serve you. I hope you find peace and tranquility during your stay."

Jordan hoped she found the 900-carat Star of the East and sufficient evidence of money laundering to hang Bartholomew Greene out to dry. The possibility she might hang his director of security alongside him was an added bonus.

A glance at her watch showed she had an hour yet before her meeting with the guru of green. Plenty of time to conduct an electronic sweep, advise headquarters she was in place and scrub away the effects of her long flight.

Plugging in the earpiece of Mackenzie's high-tech sniffer, she hummed along with Travis while she ambled through the luxurious cottage. The sweep didn't detect any devices inside the bungalow, only standard motion sensors at the windows and a security camera tucked up under the eaves of the lanai. At least Greene allowed his guests privacy inside their quarters, Jordan thought as she fought the urge to flip the bird in the direction of the camera lens.

No point in alerting TJ to the fact that she'd detected his silent sentinel. She knew where it was and could disable it when necessary. Leaning her elbows on the railing, she gazed in seeming absorption at the sea for a few moments before going into the bathroom.

It was every bit as sumptuous as the rest of the bungalow. The counters were marble, the Jacuzzi tub was big enough to sleep four, and the open, glass-block shower was fitted with cross jets that promised a decadent water massage.

Although she hadn't found any interior bugs, training and experience had Jordan turning the taps of the Jacuzzi to full blast. With the gushing water to muffle the sound of her voice, she thumbed the transmitter in her earring. The signal bounced off a secure satellite straight into OMEGA's control center.

. Claire responded within seconds, her voice soft and musical but clear enough to carry over the gurgling water.

"Cyrene here. Go ahead, Diamond."

"Just wanted to let you know I'm in place."

"Roger that. We saw there was some weather off the coast of California. How was your flight?"

"Long. Bumpy. Tiring."

"What's your status vis-à-vis the target?"

"We're still on for our first face-to-face at four o'clock local." Jordan hesitated for a moment. "I've made contact with Scott."

"Anything to report?"

"No."

She saw no need to advise Clair that the handsome bastard could still put a hitch in her step. After confirming the time frame for her next transmission, she dumped a generous helping of the resort's frangipani bath salts into the tub, stripped off and indulged in a long hot soak.

Refreshed and revived, she pulled on ecru lace briefs and a matching half-cup bra. Strappy sandals, linen slacks and a short-sleeved silk jacket in an eye-popping red gave her just the right mix of casual and professional.

Once dressed, she peeled the adhesive backing off a flat disc the size of a dime and stuck it to the underside of an Oriental ginger jar. The device was simple, an off-the-shelf bug that Mackenzie had beefed up to detect both noise and movement. It transmitted signals to Jordan's laptop, which required a special code to view. With the device in place, she used the short wait for Danny to gather her thoughts and prepare for the upcoming meeting.

The Hawaiian chattered cheerfully during the drive to the Tranquility Institute's global headquarters. Jordan listened with half an ear while checking out the approach. Manicured lawns surrounded the low, two-story building. Scattered palms rustled gently in the late-afternoon breeze. Even the roar of the sea was muted, as if in deference to the master's desire for serenity and peace.

The interior reflected the same simplicity. Potted banyans and rubber-tree plants with glossy green leaves added the only color to an airy vestibule with glass walls and a cream-colored tile floor. A receptionist greeted Jordan cheerfully and summoned the institute's business manager.

The trim, bald individual who appeared a moment later introduced himself as Duncan Myers. "I'm Mr. Greene's financial adviser. Since you've come with what sounds like an intriguing business proposal, Bartholomew asked me to sit in on your meeting."

That was fine with Jordan. The more she could

learn about Greene's operation, the better. She followed Myers to a large conference room fronted by a glass wall that encompassed an endless expanse of sea and sky.

The opposite wall, she noted with deliberately casual interest, displayed a world map. Glowing round emeralds depicted each of the Tranquility Institute's far-flung satellite cells. Home base here in Hawaii got what looked like at least fifty carats.

The sound of footsteps signaled Bartholomew Greene's arrival. Sandy haired and medium sized, the man appeared even younger than his PR photos. He wore all white—white shoes, white slacks, white safari-style shirt, probably to showcase the pendant dangling around his neck. Its gold bezel featured a square-cut emerald with a color and clarity that took Jordan's breath away.

Wrenching her gaze from the pendant, she looked into eyes almost as bright and green as the dazzling stone. Tinted contacts, she guessed as the target came forward with both hands outstretched.

"Ms. Colby. Welcome to the Tranquility Institute."

"Thank you."

"I hope you—"

Greene broke off. His welcoming smile faded. Frowning, he glanced down at their clasped hands. When he raised those startling eyes again, they held a gentle concern.

"How fortunate that you've come to me. I sense a deep hurt in you. Or is it anger?"

He squeezed her hands, his tone modulating to one of soothing assurance.

"We'll work together while you're here, shall we, and draw out your pain."

Chapter 3

Jordan managed to keep from snatching her hands free of Greene's—barely. For a startled moment she wondered if this man did indeed possess the extraordinary faculties his PR machine hyped.

Just as quickly, she dismissed the notion that he'd seen inside her head. Greene must have received a report of her confrontation with TJ, perhaps viewed a security tape of the two of them going head to head. He would have heard her anger, fed off her hurt.

It was all done with smoke and mirrors.

"I appreciate the offer, Mr. Greene," she said with a cool smile, slipping her hands free of his, "but this is a business trip. I doubt I'll have time for you to draw anything out."

"Then we'll have to make time. And please, call me Bartholomew."

With scrupulous courtesy he waved her to a round table inlaid with multicolored woods. "I've ordered tea. Or would you prefer fresh-squeezed papaya juice?"

"Tea would be fine."

It was green, of course, a fragrant blend served in delicate Chinese cups. Jordan sipped hers appreciatively while Bartholomew's financial adviser opened a manila folder and slid out the proposal she'd FedEx'ed after several long sessions with her designers.

"Bartholomew and I have studied your proposal, Ms. Colby. Or may we dispense with formalities and call you Jordan?"

"Please do."

Duncan Myers flipped through the pages of the proposal. "It's very intriguing."

No kidding! To get her foot in the door, Jordan had cut her costs to the bone and maximized the potential profit for the institute.

"You've got built-in outlets at the various Tranquility Institutes around the world," she said, gesturing toward the world map. "You also have an established mail-order business for your herbal products and healing stones. That eliminates most of the distribution costs."

Reaching into her briefcase, she produced the sketches she and her team of designers had worked up. They featured a variety of sunglasses, reading glasses and frames for prescription lenses, all with her signature butterfly done in emeralds. Many of the frames sported additional emeralds in the side stems.

With OMEGA's extensive resources to assist her, Jordan had collected a wealth of information on the supposed healing properties of emeralds. According to ancient lore, the stone was a blood detoxifier and antipoison. More current literature insisted it promoted love, romance, joy, clear vision, faith and serenity. It was also supposed to lift depression; cure insomnia; cleanse the heart, lymph nodes, blood and pancreas; restore sugar balance; ease labor and delivery; and assist in healing eyesight and speech impediments. Just your average, all-around miracle rock.

Jordan's crash course had also included detailed briefings on chakras, or the centers of energy located along the midline of the body. There were seven, running from the crown of the head to the pelvis. Various stones, she'd learned, impacted the chakras differently. Playing to that theme, she began her pitch.

"As you're aware, the emerald primarily strengthens the heart chakra. However, the stone is reputed to have positive properties for—"

"Reputed?" Greene interrupted, one brow lifting.

"Don't you believe these healing stones generate their own unique force fields?"

"Well…"

She hesitated, reluctant to come out with a flat lie. Greene would see right through it.

"All crystals and gemstones emit vibrations at different frequencies," he said, filling the small silence. "That's why we have quartz watches."

"True."

"If a stone chip can power a watch, surely it's not that big a leap to believe it can transfer its energy in other ways. Ways that help heal."

"I know many people believe in the healing power of stones," Jordan said, choosing her words carefully. "I don't question the sincerity of that belief."

Bartholomew steepled his fingers under his chin and accepted her tap dance with a smile. "Perhaps we'll make a disciple out of you while you're here."

He could try. Jordan attempted to keep an open mind regarding others' beliefs. But she figured the world wouldn't need doctors if colored stones could cure every ill and restore balance to the human body.

"As you can see," she continued, fanning the sketches across the table, "I've designed some glasses with emeralds on the right stem, some on the left."

According to her research, the left side of the body was the feminine or receptive side. Wearing a gemstone on the left drew in its energies. Wearing it on the right, or masculine side, sent the energy out to others.

"I've designed these stems to be detachable. The wearer could interchange them according to his or her needs that day."

"That's very clever," Bartholomew said with warm approval. "You might not be a believer, but you've obviously done your homework."

"Yes, I have. I also read that most men carry their stones in their pocket."

Greene patted his pendant. "I wear mine here, right over my heart."

Jordan suspected most men weren't secure enough in their beliefs—or their masculinity—to display their emeralds so openly.

"Since female clothing has fewer pockets," she continued, "women must either wear their stones as jewelry or tuck them inside their bras. Jeweled glasses would eliminate that necessity, which will make a great marketing pitch. As an added benefit, both men and women could slide the glasses up on their foreheads to get the stones closer to their head chakra."

She tipped hers up to demonstrate before drawing out an accessories page.

"Or they could dangle the glasses from one of these specially crafted chains."

Greene's face lit up as he eyed the gold links studded with tiny emeralds. "I like these."

She'd figured he would. Anything to bilk his customers of a few more bucks.

"I've researched your client base. While they tend toward the high end of the income scale, I think we should offer a wide range of prices for each line. The cost, of course, will depend on the weight, cut and clarity of the embedded stones."

Duncan Myers spoke up at that point. Sitting back in his chair, he palmed a hand over his shining bald crown.

"We can help there. Since we sell so many emeralds at our tranquility centers, I've negotiated special rates with our suppliers."

It was the perfect opening. Jordan let a note of excitement creep into her voice. "You have an in with the Colombians?"

"We do business with them, yes. And with several dealers in Russia and South Africa."

"The Colombian stones are the purest," Bartholomew put in, "although I admit I'm partial to the veining in the Zambian stones."

Yeah, Jordan thought, she'd just bet he was. Like in the Star of the East. Extracting a spreadsheet from her briefcase, she slid it across the conference table.

"I prepared detailed cost estimates and suggested retail prices for the designs you see here, but they're based on the current market price per carat. If you work me a deal with your suppliers, we can adjust the bottom line."

"You'll also need to take into consideration the fact that you're trading on Bartholomew's name and reputation," Myers commented.

"Of course. But I assure you, I've squeezed my profit margin as tight as I can."

The financial adviser made a tsk-tsking noise. "There's always room for negotiation. Let me crunch the numbers and we'll talk again."

Clearly uninterested in the nitty-gritty business detail, Bartholomew shoved back his chair. "In the meantime you can relax and enjoy some of the activities here at the institute. And I'd very much like you to attend one of our group sessions."

The tone was mild, but Jordan got the message. If she wanted to convince the guru of green to buy into her proposal for a line of pricey, emerald-studded glasses, she'd better play his game. Shrugging, she made a show of giving in.

"Why not?"

"Splendid!"

"I believe I saw a group session on the schedule for tomorrow morning. I'll join that—if you don't think I'll upset the dynamics of the group."

"Not at all," Greene assured her, beaming. "Our guests come and go all the time. One of my main goals is to help them maintain inner serenity despite the constant changes taking place around them."

Jordan gave a noncommittal nod, but the more she thought about it, the more she realized joining one of Greene's group gropes worked to her advantage. It provided an excuse to hang around the institute for a few more days and observe the natives in their natural setting. She might even be able to work in a session or two at the spa. A seaweed wrap or mud bath sounded pretty good after her bumpy flight.

"You'll join us for dinner, I hope." Greene issued the invitation with one of his disarming smiles. "Seven o'clock, in the Jade Buddha Restaurant? That will give me the opportunity to introduce you to some of our other guests."

"I'll see you then."

Despite its appellation, the Jade Buddha was more of a dining hall for the rich and famous than a restaurant. Everyone arrived at pretty much the same time and the menu posted in elegant script at each table offered only two choices—fish and vegetarian.

The fat, happy Buddha who gave the place its name sat cross-legged on a stone pedestal, surrounded by pools filled with floating lotus blossoms and magnificent koi. Guests mingled poolside while waiters served fruit-juice cocktails and passed trays of appetizers.

Greene escorted Jordan through the crowd, making introductions as they went. She shook hands with an aging movie star whose face showed the ravages of his years of substance abuse, a short, squat computer mogul and a frizzy-haired widow in a thousand-dollar St. John lounge suit paired with high-top black sneakers.

Several of the guests recognized Jordan from her modeling days. Some, like the anxious-looking mother accompanied by her ten-year-old son, were too wrapped up in their own problems to evince any interest in the newcomer's background.

"Davy's asthmatic," the thin, nervous Patricia Helms explained, her glance darting constantly to the boy. "The attacks have gotten so bad lately and the doctors can't seem to help. Dr. Greene is our last hope."

Jordan kept her opinion on that to herself and made mental notes on everyone she met. She'd have Claire run the names through OMEGA's computers. She couldn't quite envision any of these people as willing accomplices in Greene's illegal activities, but he had to get the massive amounts he was suspected of laundering off the island and into various bank accounts somehow. He could well be using his guests as unsuspecting mules.

Signaling to a passing waiter, Greene claimed two cocktails decorated with orchids and fat chunks of pineapple. He handed one to Jordan and lifted the other in salute. After the receptionist's warning about the institute's nonalcohol policy, she was prepared for the straight shot of guava juice. She wasn't prepared, though, when her host's attention zinged to the door behind her.

"Ah, good. Here's our Director of Security."

Glancing over her shoulder, she watched TJ's all-too-familiar figure stroll into the restaurant. The overhead spots highlighted the sun streaks in his brown hair and cast the strong planes of his face into sharp relief.

Greene's voice floated above the buzz of cocktail-hour conversation. "TJ! Come and meet our newest guest."

Jordan stiffened, wondering if Bartholomew was toying with her. Had he watched a tape of her earlier confrontation with TJ? Or somehow learned about their brief affair? If so, no hint of it showed in his eager, open expression.

TJ, on the other hand, looked anything but serene as he cut through the crowd. Without the mirrored sunglasses to shield his gray eyes, they seemed to slice right into Jordan.

"Ms. Colby and I have already met," he informed his employer. "Here, and in New York."

"That's right, you're both from the Big Apple!"

He said it as if living in a city with a population of more than eight million automatically qualified everyone as friends and neighbors.

"Why don't you join us. You two can catch up on old times."

TJ's glance slid to Jordan. A mocking glint flickered in those granite eyes, but his reply was preempted by the appearance of a woman who'd garnered her own share of sensational publicity.

Blond, much divorced and immensely wealthy, Felicity Dennison Albright Waller-Winston hooked her arm through TJ's. The fist-size emerald pinned to her left shoulder pressed into his bicep as she cuddled against him.

"Yes, sweetiekins," she purred, "do join us. We missed you at lunch."

"Sorry, I can't." With a polite smile, TJ disengaged. "I just came by to remind Bartholomew we're taking perimeter security down to install the new Y-beam system."

Jordan had to give Scott reluctant marks for staying on top of his profession. The Y-beam was the hottest new infrared sensor. The military had released it for commercial application only a few months ago. Mackenzie had briefed all the OMEGA operatives on the technology. She'd also assured them the new zip-up thermal suits she'd developed would shield them from Y-beams. It was looking as if Jordan would get a chance to test one out.

"How long will the system be down?" Bartholomew wanted to know.

"Less than an hour. I've got the new sensors in place and ready to activate."

With a nod for Jordan and a smile for the blonde, TJ eased his way through the milling guests. Felicity Waller-Winston swiped her tongue over heavily glossed lips and followed his progress across the room.

"That man comes darned close to making me forget I've sworn off the male of the species for the rest of my life."

So much for that right side/left side business, Jordan thought wryly. The divorcée might have her emerald pinned to her feminine, receptive side, but she was sending out decidedly assertive signals. So assertive their host questioned her about them.

"Are you troubled, Felicity?"

"No, Doc. Just horny."

Apparently that was a common condition for the woman, as her therapist didn't appear particularly surprised by the announcement.

"You're making great progress. It's necessary for you to recognize and acknowledge your feelings."

"Oh, I recognize them, all right. It's what I do about them that gets me into so much trouble."

"Why don't you try an extra half hour of meditation tonight," Greene suggested. "We'll explore your feelings in more depth during the group session tomorrow."

Jordan almost choked on her guava juice. Oh, great! That's all she needed. An hour listening to another female explore her carnal feelings for Thomas Jackson Scott.

She soon discovered the much-divorced Waller-Winston wasn't the only woman at the institute with an interest in Scott. Nudging Jordan in the ribs, the blonde directed her attention to the slender Eurasian who stopped TJ at the door.

"That's the spa director. Liana Wu. The bitch."

"Excuse me?"

"Well, look at her. She's got that tiny, porcelain-doll thing going. I refuse to stand anywhere close to the woman. She makes me look like a knob-kneed giraffe."

If Felicity towered over the spa director, Jordan would dwarf her. The possibility didn't particularly concern her. She'd long ago learned to use her five-nine height to her advantage.

"Rumor is," Felicity confided, "Liana baby is hot for our boy TJ."

No surprise there, Jordan thought in disgust. Scott had snagged *her* interest at their first meeting. Angry all over again at herself for falling for the crooked cop, she turned away.

Dinner was a long, lingering affair. Afterward, Jordan walked back to her bungalow through a scented night, stopping at a scenic overlook to prop her elbows on the trunk of a palm that curved at waist level.

The surveillance cameras she knew were scattered throughout the grounds would capture the image of a mainlander lost to the majesty of the surf foaming white against black cliffs. The ocean's roar would serve as a natural sound buffer for her report to OMEGA. Folding her arms, Jordan toyed absently with her earring. One flick activated the transmitter.

"This is Diamond."

Claire came on within a few seconds. "Cyrene here. I read you, Diamond."

Lightning chimed in as well. "I'm here, too."

The fact that her boss was still at the control center despite the late hour D.C. time didn't surprise Jordan. Not with the kind of political pressure OMEGA was facing on this mission. She gave him the names of the guests she'd met at dinner and a rundown of her earlier encounter with Greene and his financial adviser.

"They're interested. Definitely interested. Myers volunteered to get me in good with his pals in Colombia. He's going to help me work a deal on an emerald supply."

"Nice of him."

"Isn't it? I suspect he'll pocket a fat broker's fee."

"Or skim more off the top of Greene's business deals with the Colombians."

"Speaking of skimming," she said, scowling at the pinpricks of iridescent green glittering in the dark depths of the sea, "did Cyrene tell you TJ Scott was waiting for me when I arrived?"

"She did."

Lightning didn't ask the question, but Jordan answered it anyway.

"Scott still claims he was set up."

"You were there. What do you think?"

What she thought about Thomas Jackson Scott would blister the airwaves. Reining in her anger, Jordan answered as coolly as she could.

"I'm keeping him in my sights."

Five thousand miles away, Lightning shared a quick look with Cyrene. Any target Diamond got in her crosshairs was a walking corpse.

"I'm going to do some night work a little later," she told them. "Pay another visit to Greene's office. Among other things, I want to see what kind of information he gathered on Scott before hiring him."

"Keep us posted," Lightning instructed. "And be careful."

"Will do."

Cyrene cut the transmission and added a note in her electronic log, while Nick digested Diamond's report. He trusted both her skills and her instincts or he wouldn't have sent her in. As far as he knew, those instincts had failed her only once. Thoughtfully, he met Claire's glance.

"Pull up everything you can on TJ Scott. I want the names of the officers who busted him. The pimps and dealers he put the squeeze on. The judge who threw out his case. The address of his favorite pizza joint. Where he buys his underwear. *Everything.*"

Chapter 4

The black thermal suit fit Jordan like a second skin. As thin and supple as Saran, its inner lining was coated with a high-tech polymer that made the body-hugging jumpsuit easy to slither into.

The lining trapped and contained body heat, thus reducing the wearer's thermal signature and making him or her virtually undetectable by infrared scanners. That was great on missions to Alaska or Antarctica. Not so great in steamy Hawaii. Still, Jordan figured swimming around in her own sweat was a small price to pay for virtual invisibility.

Twisting her hair into a loose knot on top of her head, she dragged up the black hood and worked it around her earrings. The embedded transmitter was so sensitive she could send and receive right through the polymer coating.

Hood in place, she rolled down the attached face mask. The mouth and eye slits were covered with a breathable version of the same heat-containing shield. With every inch of her body encased in skintight black, she felt like a night version of Spider-Man.

She flicked off the bathroom lights and watched herself disappear. The wide mirror above the sink didn't pick up so much as a shadow when she moved. With the CD player/electronic sweep in hand, she let herself out a side window. She left it open behind her. She'd reenter her bungalow the same way to avoid triggering the iris-recognition system and advertising her late-night expedition.

Velvet darkness surrounded her, ripe with the scent of tropical vegetation and the salty tang of the sea. Avoiding the crushed-lava pathways, Jordan glided across the lush lawns like a silent shadow. The sniffer allowed her to pick her way through the elaborate security grid. The thermal suit deflected TJ's new Y-beams. Or so she hoped!

She reached the business center a few moments later. From her earlier visit, Jordan knew the location of the intrusion-detection devices at the windows. She zapped one with the sniffer, jimmied the lock, got the window up and was through it in thirty seconds flat. Another zap reset the electronic watchdog. The interruption would appear as a temporary blip on a monitor, if it appeared at all.

All too aware of the cameras mounted at regular intervals, Jordan kept to the shadows as she worked her way to the conference room where she'd met with Greene and Myers. The moonlight streaming through the floor-to-ceiling glass window illuminated the map depicting Greene's far-flung empire. The emerald marking the headquarters here in Hawaii gleamed like a giant eye, following her stealthy progress across the conference room and into the private offices beyond.

Two hours later, Jordan reentered her bungalow through the open window. She'd accessed the computer in Greene's office, rummaged through the files in Myers's sleek little laptop and poked into every corner of the headquarters.

To her intense disappointment, she'd uncovered nothing. Nada. Zilch-ola. No evidence of offshore bank accounts. No link to the Colombians except through legitimate purchase orders for emeralds. No hidden treasure room containing the Star of the East. She *had*, however, sweated off at least five pounds.

Dragging up the thermal suit's face mask, Jordan stopped only long enough to type a code into her laptop and verify no one had entered the bungalow in her absence before making straight for the bathroom. Every pore in her body screamed with relief when she peeled off the jumpsuit and kicked free of the clinging fabric.

In her eagerness to shed the artificial skin, Jordan put a little too much oomph into the kick. Her sweat-slick foot slipped on the tiles and went out from under her. She flung out a hand to break her fall, felt it crunch against the marble counter and landed with a thud that sucked the air from her lungs.

"Dammit!"

She flexed her hand a few times. It didn't feel as though she'd broken any bones, but she'd sport one heck of a bruise in the morning. Rolling to her feet, she stripped off her sweat-drenched panties and bra and wadded them up with the thermal suit for rinsing out later. Her next priority was a long, hot shower.

Turning the crisscrossing shower jets to full blast, she stepped inside and let the water fog up the glass blocks until a gruff shout shattered her bliss.

"Jordan!"

Cursing, she cut the jets and whipped around. Over the stair-stepping glass blocks, she got a good visual of the male who strode through the door. She swore again, yanked one of the resort's ultraplush towels from the rack, wrapped it sarong style and rounded the glass block wall.

"So much for expecting any privacy at the Tranquility Institute," she snapped. "Can any employee come waltzing into a guest's bungalow, or have you added breaking and entering to your résumé?"

He took his time replying. Jordan steamed while his gaze made a slow trip from her neck to her knees and back again. Tipping her chin, she conducted a similar inspection. He'd traded his duty uniform for a black T-shirt and well-worn jeans that hugged his muscular thighs. A cell phone was clipped to his waist. Apparently the no-phone policy didn't apply to the institute's director of security.

"The officer on duty heard what he thought was the sound of someone falling," he said, catching her gaze.

"Heard?"

Jordan stiffened. She'd swept the entire bungalow. There was no way she could have missed a bug. Not with Mackenzie's state-of-the art sniffer.

"Heard how?" she demanded.

"The bathroom tiles are pressurized to detect dropped objects weighing more than fifty pounds."

"What? Why?"

"Most hotel accidents happen in the bathroom. Usually when people are getting in or out of the tub. Since the cottages aren't equipped with phones for guests to use in case of an emergency, my predecessor devised this method of alerting us to a fall."

Involuntarily, Jordan lifted a foot. Balancing like a stork on one leg, she scowled at the decorative tiles under her other foot and scrambled to recall the type of flooring in the headquarters building.

Parquet. Both the conference room and the offices featured floor of inlaid wood. Had those floors been pressurized, too? Had TJ tracked her progress the entire time?

If so, he made no mention of it. His concern

seemed centered on the thud his security officer had heard.

"I pounded on your door. When I didn't get an answer, I did a security override and came in to check on you. From what I saw when I walked in," he added after a short, charged pause, "you look to be in pretty good shape."

Jordan's foot hit the tiles with a thump. The situation reminded her all too forcefully of the last time she'd gotten naked with this man. A whole anticorruption squad had busted through the door on that occasion.

"Okay, Scott. You did your duty and checked things out. You can leave now."

"Not yet. Did you fall?"

"Yes, I fell."

"What happened?"

"What do you think? I slipped on the tiles and took a dive. Now, if you don't mind…"

She waved a hand to send him on his way. He stood his ground, obviously not ready to be dismissed.

"I need to fill out an accident report. What caused you to slip?"

She could hardly tell him her nocturnal prowling in the equivalent of a portable steam room left her dripping with sweat down to and including her feet.

"I got in the shower. Stepped out to fetch the shampoo. Lost my footing on the wet tiles and went down. After which, I got back in the shower where I remained until I was so rudely interrupted."

She should have remembered he was a cop. One of the best, they'd told her, before he'd turned. His glance zeroed in on the array of toiletries in the basket on the marble vanity. Each bore the resort's exclusive label—including the mango scented shampoo.

Hiking up the bath towel, Jordan moved to block his view of the shower stall. For all he knew, she'd used her own personal brand of suds.

"Look, Scott, I've had a long day and I'm—"

"Well, hell! You really did a number on yourself."

His gaze had dropped to the middle of her chest. Glancing down, Jordan saw a mottled bruise already forming on the hand gripping the towel.

"It's nothing. I just hit my hand on the counter when I went down."

He crossed the room in two strides. "Better let me take a look at that."

"Hey! Do you mind? I'm naked here."

"Yeah, I noticed. Give me your hand, Red."

And release her death grip on the towel? Jordan didn't think so.

"What are you going to do?" she jeered. "Kiss the boo-boo and make it better?"

His grin slipped out then, the same crooked grin that had once put a flutter in Jordan's stomach. To her profound disgust, it still generated a few quivers.

"The NYPD first responder's medical training didn't include kissing as a treatment option," he said, his eyes glinting, "but I'm certainly willing to give it a shot."

Enough was enough. Jordan had to get the man out of the bathroom. And she'd damn well better do it before he noticed the thermal suit wadded up in the corner. Conceding this skirmish with something less than graciousness, she jerked her chin toward the door.

"Wait for me in the other room. I'll dry off, throw on a robe and join you there."

When TJ retreated to the sitting room, every one of his instincts had clicked into high gear. Right along with his libido.

Grimacing at the heat Jordan had stirred in his belly, he stared through the open shutters at the dark, restless sea. He'd tried to play it cool, had done his best to keep things professional, but the sight of her almost naked had blown just about every one of his circuits.

With his brain recording the erotic details and his blood making a quick trip south, TJ was surprised he'd picked up on her lie. He didn't know why she'd fed him the line about the shampoo, but his gut told him it was just that. The untouched bottle on the vanity, paired with her too-casual move to block his view of the shower stall, would have been sufficient to rouse his suspicions.

Then there was the bundle on the floor of Jordan's bathroom. He'd almost missed it, caught only a glimpse as he turned away. One glimpse was enough to raise another red flag. That bundle sure looked like a wet suit, one that had been recently worn. But the on-duty security officer reported Jordan hadn't left her cottage since returning from dinner.

The suspicion that was second nature to a cop took over from the man still sporting a hard bulge in his jeans. What the hell was Jordan up to? Why had she picked Bartholomew Greene as a potential business partner just weeks after he'd hired a new director of security? Was she out for revenge, plotting to drag TJ into the gutter the way he'd once dragged her?

The memory of that made him cringe inside. What a mess! Scrubbing a hand over the back of his neck, he stared out at the inky darkness.

He still didn't know how it had happened. All he'd intended was a few hours in the leggy ex-model's company. That night at the charity event, the Sunday afternoon in Central Park, the invitation to drive up to Connecticut for the weekend... All orchestrated to finesse the intriguing, intoxicating Jordan Colby into bed.

He certainly hadn't planned on becoming as fascinated with her mind as he was with her sensuous body. Nor had he figured on moving with lightning speed from plain old-fashioned lust to something harder to define. And he sure as hell had never dreamed Jordan would be in his bed when officers from his own precinct busted down his door.

The swish of cloth slippers on carpet told him

Jordan had finished in the bathroom. Slamming the door on his memories, TJ turned. She'd wrapped her hair in a towel turban and belted on one of the resort's monogrammed robes. It took everything he had not to think about what was under that thick, white terry cloth.

"You don't need to play doc," she said dismissively. "My hand is fine."

"There's a slight matter of liability at stake here. Let's see it."

"I'm not going to sue the institute."

"Let's see it."

Taking her hand in a light hold, he performed a visual inspection. She'd hit the edge of her hand, just below the little finger. The bruise was already an ugly red and purpling fast, but he didn't spot any swelling, protrusions or awkward joint angles that would indicate a fracture or dislocation.

"How bad does it hurt?"

"It doesn't. Much."

Gently TJ manipulated her little finger. When it moved freely without a wince or a grunt on Jordan's part, he tested the metacarpal, the wrist and her lower arm.

"Doesn't feel like you broke any bones. Let's see your other hand."

With an air of impatience she didn't bother to disguise, she placed her left hand in his. TJ compared the two and saw no glaring distortion in their shape or size, aside from the discoloration.

"I prescribe an ice pack and ibuprofen if it starts to throb. You want to avoid aspirin because it—"

"Because it slows clotting. Thanks, I know how to treat bruises."

TJ gave her a considering look. "Sustained a lot of them, have you?"

He'd always wondered about the scar above her eyebrow. The cop in him had also noted how neatly she would sidestep any reference to her childhood in their admittedly brief hours together. She'd shrugged off his questions then and did the same now.

"Obviously you've never been behind the scenes at a fashion show. Backstage is nothing short of controlled chaos. With just minutes to make a complete wardrobe change, models are always bumping into dressers, makeup artists or each other. I had to cover up more than one bruise over the years."

Jordan delivered that last statement without blinking an eye. It was true. Truer than he would ever know. She was battling memories she refused to let surface when TJ raised her hand to his lips.

The kiss was as light as the touch of snow, but the contact jolted through her with the impact of a Taser. So did the glint of laughter in his eyes.

"All better now?"

"Yes." Jerking her hand free of his, she shoved it into the pocket of her terry cloth robe. "Good night."

He took the hint. Finally! Relieved she would be rid of him, Jordan trailed him to the entryway.

"I'll check on you tomorrow," he told her at the door. "If there's any swelling or stiffness in the finger joint, we'd better take you into town for X-rays."

She frowned up at him, struck by the absolute absurdity of the situation. She hadn't exactly led a sedate life before *or* after being recruited by OMEGA. More than one of her undercover assignments had required her to dodge bullets and/or bounce off walls.

Just last year she'd dangled helplessly at the end of a helicopter retrieval cable, slamming into sheer canyon walls while the crew worked frantically to compensate for a sudden downdraft and reel her in. The year before, she'd cracked a rib leaping from one rooftop to another in pursuit of a Swiss forger.

That TJ would make such a big deal about one little pinkie both annoyed and disturbed Jordan. She wasn't used to people fussing over her. Especially rogue cops who topped her shortlist of suspects in a possible money-laundering scheme.

"I'll let you know if the hand bothers me. Good night."

He tipped her a salute and departed. Jordan stood at the door for a moment, listening to the soft crunch of his footsteps on the lava walkway, watching him move through the tropical night. As he merged with the shadows, her gaze swept the postcard-perfect scene.

A fat moon hung low above the mountains,

washing their jagged peaks with pale light. The dark silhouettes of palm trees stood like tall sentinels against the night sky. Their fronds rustled in the breeze, as if whispering secrets to the waves curling against the cliffs.

It was a setting designed for romance. A night made for lovers. Jordan didn't realize she was rubbing the spot TJ had kissed until she pressed the bruise a little too hard.

"Idiot," she muttered, thoroughly disgusted with herself.

One crooked grin. That's all it had taken to breach her barriers again. She knew what the man was. Knew what he'd done. Yet here she was, tingling like some silly schoolgirl from his touch.

"Idiot," she said again and slammed the door on the magical night.

What she needed, Jordan decided, was a long, hard workout at the spa. She'd schedule one for tomorrow, after the group session Greene had talked her into. And that seaweed wrap, she thought, re-membering Felicity Waller-Winston's sly comment about the spa director. If the dark-haired Eurasian had gotten as close to TJ as Felicity had hinted, Jordan might be able to worm some information about him and their mutual employer out of the woman.

The plan should have sparked a sense of antici-pation. Instead, the idea of pumping Liana Wu for intimate details about TJ left almost as sour a taste in Jordan's mouth as the prospect of listening to Felicity go into detail about her horny state.

Her mouth curling, she retrieved a towel from the bathroom, yanked a tray of ice cubes from the mini-fridge and slapped an ice pack over her injured hand.

How the hell did she do it?

His jaw tight, TJ cut across the grounds to the building that housed the security center.

How the hell did the woman tie him in knots every time he got within five feet of her?

Granted, a man would have to be dead from the neck down not to react to the sight that had greeted TJ when he'd entered the steam-filled bathroom. He suspected the erotic image would keep him awake for most of the night. That and the fact that Jordan had lied to him.

Still puzzling over her slip about the shampoo, TJ let himself in through the rear door of the administrative center. With its wide porch, green shutters and high, hipped roof, the building blended in with the turn-of-the-century style of the other structures. The offices inside, however, were equipped with the best that money could buy.

Housekeeping and personnel took up one wing, maintenance another. TJ's domain included offices for him and his second in command, a locker room and break area for his staff of thirty, an administrative area and the ops center lined with banks of monitors.

There was also an armory stocked with a lethal assortment of weapons. TJ insisted his people hone their skills regularly at the firing range. The wealthy, high-profile guests who sequestered themselves at the Tranquility Institute made too tempting a target for stalkers or kidnappers.

The security officer working the 7:00 a.m. to 2:00 a.m. shift looked up when his boss entered. "How's Ms. Colby?"

"You pegged it. She did take a fall."

"She okay?"

"She hit her hand going down, but I don't think she broke any bones."

TJ snagged a cup of coffee from the pot his security crew kept perking twenty-four-seven. The sludge looked like something pumped out by an exhaust pipe and was probably ninety-nine percent caffeine, but he didn't figure he'd get much sleep tonight anyway.

"You've got the incident recorded in your log, right?"

"Yes, sir." The officer used a mouse to scroll down the electronic log. "Right here."

TJ scanned the lines and was about to signal his approval, when a brief entry just above caught his attention. Frowning, he leaned over the officer's shoulder.

"What's this?"

"One of the intrusion-detection devices at the main business center went down. It came right back up again, but I made a note for maintenance to test the system first thing in the morning."

"Show me which device."

A click of the mouse brought up the business center's security grid. Another click tagged the device protecting one of the first-floor windows.

"Did you direct the cameras to sweep that area?"

"Yes, sir, as soon as the device went down."

"Pull up the sweep," TJ instructed, a tight feeling in his gut. "I want to see it."

Chapter 5

The morning group gathered in a large, airy room at the Meditation Center. Outside, a tropical shower pattered down on broad-leafed palms and banyans. Inside, fans whirled lazily, drawing in the spongy scent of wet earth.

Jordan had taken her cue from the casual resort attire she'd observed last night. Comfortable in jeweled flip-flops, gauzy white drawstring shorts and a shimmering turquoise halter top by one of New York's top designers, she settled into a high-backed rattan chair and surveyed the others gathered for the session.

Felicity Waller-Winston lounged in the chair opposite Jordan's. Her blond hair was scraped back from her face and caught with a band, making her look both older and unhappier in the harsh light of day. Her arms and shoulders were bare, her breasts flattened by a stretchy bandeau top. She held her emerald in her hand and thumbed it constantly with a twitchy stroke.

Edna Albert, the widow Jordan had met last night, sat next to Felicity. Barely five-one or -two, the frizzy-haired matron looked lost in the oversize fan-back chair. Her emerald dangled from a gold chain looped around her neck. Like Felicity, she worked her thumb over the stone.

The ten-year-old asthmatic, Davy Helms, claimed the seat next to Edna's. *His* thumbs skimmed over the controls of a Game Boy.

The other three attendees eyed Jordan with varying degrees of curiosity, but Bartholomew's arrival preempted introductions. His first order of business was to offer Jordan a glistening green teardrop threaded with a gold chain.

"Ideally, everyone should select his or her own stone. It's a very personal choice that must come from the heart. I've had this beautiful gem in my private collection for some time, though, and thought of it the moment I touched your hands yesterday."

He dropped the emerald into her palm and made a clucking sound at the contrast between the stone's shimmering purity and the ugly purple bruise marring her skin.

"TJ gave me a report of your accident."

Jordan wasn't surprised. She suspected Greene's director of security kept him apprised of everything that went on at the institute. Including, she couldn't help wondering, that touching, tender kiss?

She'd spent hours last night reliving Scott's sudden appearance in her bathroom, dissecting his every word, remembering the warmth of his lips against her skin. Annoyed that she could still feel a tingle, she shrugged aside her host's concern.

"The bruise looks worse than it feels. This stone is magnificent."

Her deliberate attempt to change the topic worked. Greene almost purred as he closed her fingers gently over the emerald teardrop.

"It's one of the finer samples from our friends at the Muzo mine. My gemologist has had it soaking in saltwater since yesterday afternoon to release its healing properties. Perhaps you'll feel its energy during our session."

Or not, Jordan thought as he took his seat and opened the session. After introducing her to the group, he went around the circle and invited the others to provide whatever information about themselves they felt comfortable sharing.

Jordan picked up a wealth of detail on each guest. She also learned more than she wanted to know about Edna's four ungrateful daughters and Felicity's vigorous sex life. When it was her turn, she supplied her name and the fact that she was visiting the institute on business.

Edna squinted across the room. "So what's your problem, sweetie?"

"I don't have one. I'm merely here to listen and learn how best to satisfy the needs of Bartholomew's clients in the line of glasses I'm proposing to sell through the institute's outlets."

"Bull crackers," the widow snorted, crossing one sneakered foot over the other. "Everyone has problems. You just don't want to talk about yours."

Bartholomew intervened with a mild reproof. "Now, Edna. You know how group works. No one is required to speak if they don't wish to. Do you all have your stones?"

Hands went to pockets and to necklines. Emeralds of every size, shape and clarity appeared.

"Good. We'll begin with five minutes of meditation. Take a deep breath. Release it. Again…"

Like obedient children, the other six members of the group followed his instructions. Jordan snuck a glance at each of them as chests rose and fell.

"Now think about your physical state," Greene murmured, stroking his pendant with a lover's caress. "Concentrate on the way you're sitting. Whether you're warm or cool. Are you full from breakfast or ready for lunch?"

Edna closed her eyes. Felicity dropped her head against the rattan chair back and let her gaze drift toward the ceiling. Ten-year-old Davy hunched his shoulders, swung his legs and stared at the floor.

Jordan went with the flow. Thankful that Claire's

pre-brief had prepared her for this sort of hocus-po-
cus, she closed her eyes.

"Shift your attention to your feelings," Greene
said after several silent moments. "Don't judge.
Don't analyze. Just let the sensations come and go,
bringing thoughts and memories and associations."

Jordan didn't have any trouble identifying her
feelings. Impatience ranked right up there at the
top, although she had to admit the man had a mes-
merizing voice.

"Now expand your focus. Bring in the world around
you. Do you hear the rain on the roof? Feel the ocean
breeze against your skin? Let the sounds and colors
and shapes come to you. Broaden you. Stimulate you."

Okay, this wasn't so bad. Head cocked, Jordan
found herself listening to the rhythm of the rain and
breathing in the tang of the sea.

"Relax," Greene said in a seductive whisper.
"Relax. Your body. Your mind. Become one with
your world. Your self."

Sneaking a peak, Jordan saw that several of the
other guests appeared to have achieved a near-hyp-
notic state. Edna's mouth sagged open, showing a
good deal of expensive bridgework. Felicity was
gazing dreamily up at the ceiling.

"Who wants to begin?" Greene asked softly.
"Who's feeling an increased perceptual sensitivity?"

Felicity let out a gusty sigh. "I'm feeling an increased something, Doc, but I wouldn't classify it
as perceptual."

Edna's mouth snapped shut. Her eyes popped open. With a cackling snort, she sat up in her fan-shaped chair.

"Hooo, boy! Here we go. Miss Hot Pants is going to tell again about how she can only achieve spiritual fulfillment with a stud."

Jordan shot a look at the youngest member of the group. Surely Greene wouldn't allow Felicity to give the graphic details about her erotic cravings in the presence of a ten-year-old.

He didn't, thank goodness. With deft skill, the therapist led Felicity into an exploration of her seemingly deep-seated belief that a physical relationship was the only kind she believed she could have with a man. By the time the much-divorced blonde admitted she couldn't trust any male to love her more than her bank account, she was sobbing, Edna was clucking in sympathy, and the tip of Jordan's borrowed emerald was gouging into her palm.

Frowning, she eased her grip on the stone. Evidently she had more in common with Felicity Waller-Winston than she would have imagined. She'd trust every member of the OMEGA team—male or female—with her life, but ice would coat this tropical paradise before she'd trust *anyone* with her heart again. Especially ex-cops with hard eyes and a touch so gentle her injured hand still tingled with the memory of it.

The emerald dug deeper, vying with the bruise for

attention. She used the pain to keep focused on her reason for joining this little psycho-circle. When the session finally ended and Jordan tried to return the stone, Bartholomew insisted she hang on to it.

"Wear it you while you're here. You may get attached to it," he added with a mischievous grin, "and add to the institute's profits by making a purchase."

"I may," she agreed, slipping the chain over her head. With the green teardrop nestled between her breasts, she took advantage of the opening he'd just offered her. "But as you said, the choice of a stone is a very personal matter. I'd like to test some others. Perhaps I'll feel their energy more directly."

"Of course!" Beaming at the possibility of a convert, Bartholomew pulled a small laminated schedule from his shirt pocket. "I have private sessions scheduled before and after lunch and another group at three. Why don't you join me at my residence for drinks before dinner and I'll show you my private collection."

"I'd like that."

Very much!

"Shall we say sixish?"

"Sixish works for me."

Jordan used the rest of the morning to explore the resort's facilities and talk with as many of the guests and staff as possible without appearing too inquisitive. Her casual inquiries confirmed the surface impression of a superbly run and extremely profitable operation. The only hint of anything unusual came during lunch.

It was an elaborate affair, served poolside by waiters in flowery Hawaiian shirts and waitresses in long, flowing muumuus. Another shower pattered against the protective overhang as guests helped themselves to a buffet of fresh fruit, exotic salads and downright sinful pastries. Jordan indulged in a generous helping of lobster salad and was debating between a meringue swan and a star-shaped kiwi tart when the short, squat computer mogul she'd met at dinner last night appeared at her elbow. The bulldog folds of his fleshy face creased into a smile at Jordan's dilemma.

"Take one of each," he suggested. "According to the staff, they're all no-cal."

"Uh-huh. And if you believe that…"

Her mind clicked up the data she'd gathered on Harry McShay. Thirty-six and a billionaire several times over, he'd lost his wife and only child to a boating accident. Two years after the tragic event, he was still reportedly haunted by their deaths.

Grief hadn't dulled his business acumen, though. Loading his plate with the supposedly no-cal goodies, he directed a shrewd glance at Jordan. "I understand you're proposing a line of eyewear to be sold through the Tranquility Institute's network."

"That's right."

"I have the same kind of arrangement with the

meditation software one of my subsidiaries developed for Bartholomew. Made millions off that program. Pain in the ass, though, working with Myers."

"Why?"

"The man's a shark. He'll devour you whole if you don't protect yourself. I wouldn't do business with him at all except for Bartholomew."

McShay's gaze went to the sun attempting to burn through the misty rain. Whatever he saw there added a gruff edge to his voice when he addressed Jordan again.

"Bartholomew Greene is the only reason I get up in the morning. He's worth whatever price I have to pay."

The hairs on the back of Jordan's neck tingled. She sensed McShay was talking about more than the Tranquility Institute's exorbitant fees, but before she could probe deeper Edna and two other guests joined them. When McShay drifted away, Jordan made a mental note to corner the man again later.

First she intended to corner Liana Wu. In addition to her duties as spa director, the slender, exotic Wu specialized in Aquarius salt glows. Jordan figured she might as well pump the woman while exfoliating under a mask of ocean salts, essential oils and green algae.

The spa was a tropical Eden brought indoors. Fountains splashed. Fish swam in pools that meandered through stands of bamboo. Muted Hawaiian chants, stone tiki gods and ginger incense stroked the senses the moment a guest opened the emerald green doors.

A smiling attendant greeted Jordan, confirmed her appointment and escorted her through the facility. The exercise room was a jungle of gleaming steel, with enough treadmills and stair-step machines to whip the 82nd Airborne into shape. The salon boasted six stations and an assortment of expensive hair and skin products. Steam rooms, hot tubs, whirlpools and a lap pool shimmering in turquoise completed the workout area.

The treatment rooms formed a semicircle at the rear of the facility. Each faced the exterior, so the guest could enjoy spectacular views of verdant peaks and rolling waves while being pumiced, pummeled or prepped. The attendant led Jordan to one of the cubicles and drew a batik wrap from the bamboo cabinet.

"I'll let Ms. Wu know you're here. She'll be right with you."

Jordan took a few moments to poke around the cubicle before shaking out the wrap. She was reaching for the drawstring on her shorts when the door opened once more. It wasn't the attendant or Liana Wu who entered, however, but TJ Scott.

He was in his duty uniform again—crisp slacks, emerald green polo shirt imprinted with the Tranquility Institute logo—but his expression conveyed none of the warmth and cheerful friendliness displayed by other members of the staff.

"Don't you ever knock?" Jordan asked, seriously annoyed.

"I want to talk to you."

"We said all that needed saying yesterday."

"Not quite. Where were you last night?"

"I beg your pardon?"

"I saw the wet suit wadded up on your bathroom floor. Did you go out for a swim?"

"Maybe I did. Is that against the rules?"

"No. The thing is, our computers indicate you went in through the front door only once last night, when you returned from dinner."

"That doesn't give me a great deal of confidence in your hot-dog system. Does it fail regularly?"

"This is the first time. *If,* in fact, it failed, which I don't believe happened." His eyes drilled into her, granite hard, stone cold. "Why did you bypass the system, Red? Where did you go?"

"What I do and where I go is my business, Scott. Yours is to protect Bartholomew Greene and his guests. It's just my opinion, of course, but it sounds like you're doing a piss-poor job of it."

He let that zing by him and kept his gaze narrowed on Jordan's face. "How did you keep your name out of the papers?"

The sudden shift caught her off guard. "What?"

"When I was arrested. The media had a field day skewering me from all sides. Yet your name never appeared on either the police blotter or the press releases put out by the NYPD, much less in the tabloids. Why?"

"I had a good lawyer."

And she worked for one of the most powerful men in the country. OMEGA's director had a direct line to the White House. Nick Jensen didn't use it often. When he did, the call produced instant results.

Her pat answer rubbed TJ the wrong way. His jaw tight, he issued a terse warning. "Listen to me, Red. I don't know what your game is or why you showed up at the Tranquility Institute just a few short weeks after I signed on, but this isn't the time or the place to fix what went wrong in New York."

It took a moment for the implications to sink in. When they did, she hooted in derision.

"You think I flew to Hawaii hoping to pick up where we left off three years ago? Hardly!"

His mask slipped for a moment. She caught a glimpse of the frustration and impatience behind it as he thrust a hand through his hair, shagging it into short brown spikes.

"Just give me a yes or no. Did you leave your bungalow last night after you got back from dinner?"

"No."

She was good. Damn good. TJ didn't know how she managed to infuse just the right mix of disdain, disgust and annoyance into a single syllable, but the woman had the combination down pat.

Problem was, he didn't believe her now any more than he had last night. This made twice that she'd lied to him, and the why of it was gnawing at his insides.

TJ had reviewed last night's security videotapes until his head pounded and the grainy images had blurred. He'd also run a physical sweep of the entire business center. If someone *had* penetrated the facility, they'd left no evidence behind.

And if that someone was Jordan, she was playing a very dangerous game. Until he figured out what that game was, he intended to keep her front and center on his internal radar screen.

"Bartholomew advised me that he plans to show you his private collection later."

She blinked at the terse pronouncement, obviously trying to follow the sharp turns in his questioning.

"Why did he advise you? Does he require your permission or approval to show off his goodies?"

"No, but he does need me to add you to the temporary access list for entry into the vault." He waited a beat, watching for her reaction. "I'll have you on the monitors every second you're inside."

"Thanks for the warning. If I decide to lift any of Bartholomew's emeralds, I'll be sure to turn my back to the cameras."

"You do that, Red."

TJ's glance dropped to the teardrop nestled between her breasts. Like the others in Greene's private collection, the emerald had been treated with a chemical compound visible only when viewed through special filters. The insurance company required the chemical paint for tracking purposes. If Jordan—or anyone else—tried to leave the institute with a stone that hadn't been washed of its special coating, she'd light up like the high beams on a semi.

TJ almost hoped she would. He could nail her then, make her answer the questions she'd dodged so skillfully up to this point. Every cop knew ways to force unwilling suspects to talk, some legal, a few close to the edge. The way he felt right now, he wouldn't mind getting Jordan Colby alone in a small, confined interrogation room.

He was deep into that scenario when Liana Wu appeared at the door to the treatment room. Her curious glance went from TJ to Jordan and back again.

"Excuse me. Am I interrupting?"

"No," he answered. "We're finished."

For now.

Chapter 6

In preparation for her visit to Bartholomew's private residence, Jordan traded her shorts and halter for a strapless sundress with a shirred bodice. The elasticized fabric clung to her breasts, leaving the rest of the white-on-white print to fall in soft folds to midcalf. The dress was sophisticatedly simple and provided the perfect foil for the emerald teardrop clasped around her neck.

The bulky, cheerful Danny appeared in his golf cart to transport Jordan to Greene's private retreat. The house sat in isolated splendor, separated from the main part of the compound by a bend in the coastline. Although the two-story residence conformed to the same plantation-style architecture as the rest of the institute, the lanai at its rear was sharp and angular and jutted out above the cliffs like the prow of a ship. Like the master of a sailing vessel, Bartholomew Greene could stand on that balcony and soak in an unobstructed view of the vast, ever-changing Pacific.

Given what TJ had imparted earlier that afternoon about the security surrounding Greene's private collection, Jordan wasn't surprised to find Duncan Myers had also been invited to the showing. The sharp-eyed business manager could no doubt tell her the exact size, shape, weight and clarity of every stone in the vault.

Myers was waiting with Bartholomew in a living room dominated by a soaring cathedral ceiling and the prow-shaped windows. The furnishings were minimal, the dimensions of the room huge, leaving an overall feeling of spaciousness.

"I have good news," Myers said after a houseboy served them all frothy, nonalcoholic cocktails. "I contacted our account rep at the Muzo mine to let him know about your proposal and see what kind of a deal he could give us."

Us, Jordan noted with great interest. Myers obviously expected a cut of whatever arrangement she worked out with his supplier over and above the profit-sharing percentages she'd laid out in her proposal.

"Alejandro and his associates had planned to make a delivery next week, but he's moved his trip up so he could meet with you while you're here."

How accommodating of the Colombians to alter their schedule on her account. Jordan downed a sip of her juice to slow her suddenly racing pulse.

"When do they arrive?"

"The day after tomorrow. Alejandro said he'd bring a supply of stones suitable for the frames you've proposed."

"I've dealt with Alejandro Garcia for more than a decade," Bartholomew commented. "He knows as much or more about emeralds as anyone in the business."

Jordan logged the name into her memory bank. She'd have to get Claire working on the man, like fast.

"He supplied many of the stones I'm going to show you," Greene said as he escorted her into his private lair.

The study exuded the same tranquil air as of the rest of the residence. Wide windows took up one wall. Fitted with retractable screens to block the glare, they framed a stunning view of Ma'aona, the holy mountain. Bookshelves painted a creamy white stretched from floor to ceiling along the other three walls. Interspersed among the hundreds of volumes were photos of Bartholomew posing with presidents, kings and rock stars.

Including, Jordan saw with a swift, indrawn breath, a shot of her host with the sultan and sultana of D'han. Cradling her cocktail, she meandered over for a closer look.

"Now, that's an emerald worthy of a queen."

Bartholomew came to stand beside her. "The Star of the East," he murmured. "There's not another stone like it in the world."

Side by side, they eyed the glistening nine hundred carats.

"I tried to buy the Star from Omar's father," her host admitted, "then from Omar himself when he inherited the throne. Unfortunately, he insisted on keeping it to give Barbara as a wedding present. Now," he added with a sigh, "it's gone."

Watching him out of the corner of her eye, Jordan pumped him for information. "From what I read in the papers, the theft was extraordinarily well planned and executed. Whoever was behind it knew exactly what he wanted and went after it with ruthless determination."

"That's why I guard my treasures with such zealousness."

Pulling a leather-bound volume of the works of an obscure Chinese philosopher from the bookshelf, Greene blinked into a small round scanner. The shelves slid to the side on silent skids, revealing a narrow corridor blocked by a steel door.

"If you'll wait here a moment, I'll enter the necessary access codes."

Myers lingered beside Jordan at the entrance to the corridor and swiped a palm over his high-domed forehead in what she was coming to recognize as a characteristic gesture.

"This vault rates higher than most banks on the Insurance Service Office scale," he told her.

She believed it. Halon fire-suppression nozzles dotted the ceiling. Red laser beams crisscrossed to form a tight grid. Hidden motion, heat and sound sensors no doubt augmented the surveillance cameras bristling behind protective steel screens. The certainty that TJ was watching her every move raised prickly little goose bumps on Jordan's arms when the steel door swung open and Bartholomew beckoned to her.

She expected a sterile vault with rows of steel drawers, each requiring its own access code. What she stepped into was a treasure room.

"My God!"

Lighted display cases lined the walls. Inside the cases were collections of silver chalices, jeweled fans, bishops' miters and other art objects, all studded with emeralds. An ostrich-size Fabergé egg sat on a gold stand encrusted with diamonds. The egg had been carved from a clouded Russian emerald that must have weighed more than two hundred carats.

Table-style cases displayed jewelry of every style and era. Jordan's glance skimmed over what looked like an authentic gold-and-emerald Egyptian collar, a tiara that might have graced the powdered wig of a Hapsburg empress and an assortment of bracelets, rings and brooches any museum director would have killed for.

The centerpiece of the collection was contained in a lighted case given solitary prominence on the far wall. It was a massive gold crucifix hung from a chain of gold links as thick as a man's finger. The dozen or so emeralds studding the cross were magnificent. Jordan estimated the center stone at close to a hundred carats. It wasn't the size of the stones that drew her awed gaze, though, but their clarity and brilliance.

"That's the Cross of the Andes," Greene said with quiet reverence. "It was recovered from the *Santa Ignacia,* a Spanish galleon that sank off the Florida Keys in 1622."

"I read about that. Weren't the treasures found aboard her auctioned off at Christie's?"

"Most of them."

"Bartholomew financed the *Santa Ignacia's* salvage operation," Myers explained as Greene keyed in a cipher and opened the display case. "He claimed the Cross as his share of the proceeds."

Greene removed the heavy piece and cradled it in both hands. "According to legend, an Inca prince had it crafted as a gift for the king of Spain. The Spanish governor of Peru cut the prince's throat and sent the gift in his own name."

"Nice guy."

"Lay your palm over the center stone. Now close your eyes and breathe deeply. Again. Don't think. Don't analyze. Let your senses take you."

Jordan played along, breathing through her nose,

thinking that Greene really got carried away with this stuff. Suddenly her eyes popped open.

"Did you feel them?" Bartholomew asked.

She'd felt *something*. Her skin still tingled where it came in contact with the surface of the gem.

"Them?" she echoed, frowning.

"The tears of the Incas. They weep for their lost prince."

It was the power of suggestion, Jordan decided. The hypnotic quality of Bartholomew's voice coupled with the green glow from his display cases. That was the only rationale she could come up with for the odd sensation that seemed to be increasing in intensity.

"I sensed the same sorrow in you the first time we met," her host said, fixing his penetrating eyes on her. "Do you weep for someone you've lost, Jordan? A relative? A friend? A lover?"

She fought a suddenly smothering need to yank her hand back, break the connection and kill the strange vibrations. Refusing to give in to the superstitious urge, she smiled at Greene.

"You're very perceptive, Bartholomew. The first time we met, I *was* thinking of someone I'd lost."

She flicked a glance at the security camera angled for a clear shot of her face. When she brought her gaze back to Greene, her smile was razor sharp.

"But I never wept for him. He wasn't worth my tears."

* * *

Inside the Security Operations Center, TJ stood with his legs spread and his arms folded. His gaze was locked on one of the monitors fed by the six surveillance cameras inside Greene's private vault. Jordan's voice came through the speakers clear and undistorted. So clear, each word cut into TJ with the sharp, clean slice of a scalpel.

His face impassive, he said nothing as he and the on-duty officer tracked every move of the three people inside the vault. Neither of them would breathe easy until Bartholomew escorted his guests out of the vault and reactivated the redundant alarms, although for very different reasons.

Greene kept a cool fifteen million in artifacts, jewelry and gems inside that concrete-and-steel bunker. All of it had been acquired legally, or so the insurance documents and transfer certificates alleged. TJ had verified every item on the inventory personally when he'd assumed responsibility for security and again during scheduled maintenance and system tests.

Not that Bartholomew listed all his treasures on the inventory. Unknown to his employer, TJ had tracked down the original architects, obtained a set of drawings and compared them to the schematics currently on file. Sometime between design and installation, several small compartments had been added to the vault. Compartments not even the chief of security was supposed to know about.

TJ had already taken a look inside those compartments. He'd found all kinds of interesting objects,
including a World War II–era cipher stone and an
emerald phallus large enough to service a bull
elephant, but not what he was looking for.

He fully intended to go back in for another
more thorough search, but Jordan's unexpected
arrival—and unexplained activities—had put a
crimp in those plans. Not to mention a severe dent
in his ego.

He wasn't worth my tears.

The scathing comment bounced around inside
TJ's head as he watched her join Bartholomew at a
cabinet fitted with velvet-lined drawers. The drawers
held Greene's collection of loose stones, catego-
rized by size, cut and color.

"This is one of my favorites."

Bartholomew selected a heart-shaped emerald
from its velvet nest and rubbed his thumb across its
faceted surface. His eyes drifted shut. A dreamy expression came over his face. Making a low, throaty
sound, he caressed the stone with the same sensual
deliberation another man might stroke his mistress.

TJ's gaze zeroed in on Jordan. He thought he saw
a flicker of revulsion cross her face. Or maybe it was
derision. Whatever the emotion, it was gone when
Bartholomew opened his eyes and offered her the
stone.

"Try this one. See if it speaks to you."

She hesitated, reluctant to take the shimmering

green heart. TJ didn't blame her. Bartholomew had practically ejaculated on the damn thing.

Instead, she curled a hand around the teardrop dangling from the thin gold chain.

"You know, I think you might have been right this morning. I didn't give this stone a chance. I'm starting to get attached to it."

"I was *sure* that was the right stone for you!" Pleased with her choice, Greene restored the heart to its velvet pocket. "You said you didn't cry over this lost love. If you let it, the teardrop will weep for you and ease the pain you carry inside your heart."

"It's not pain," she said, lifting her chin to speak to the camera. "It's disgust."

TJ stood stiff legged and tight jawed while the trio left the vault and the steel door whirred shut behind them. One by one, the alarms reactivated. His on-duty officer ran the checklist. When the last of the redundant systems came online, the retired cop blew out a breath.

"All systems up, boss. We're back in business." After noting the time in the computerized security log, he swiveled around in his chair. "I'm stuck here for another six hours. What are you doing with the rest of the night?"

The question was innocent. Far too innocent. With a sudden prickle between his shoulder blades, TJ turned.

"Why?"

The man's mouth cocked into a grin. "The guys

on night shift have a pool going. So far the odds are on Liana Wu, but I may transfer my bet to that hot piece of tail in bungalow seven. The woman practically crawled all over you at the Jade Buddha last night."

"Ms. Waller-Winston is a guest. Don't ever let me hear you refer to her in those terms again."

Genial and slightly overweight, the officer took the reprimand with good grace.

"No, sir." His brows waggled. "So what *are* you going to do tonight?"

TJ snorted. You could take a cop out of the uniform but you could never take the morbid curiosity out of the cop.

"Well, I'll tell you," he drawled, still feeling the bite of Jordan's words. "I'm thinking about taking a bottle down to the beach and getting plastered."

Revved from her session in the vault and the news that Greene's Colombian contact was making a visit to the institute, Jordan had to swallow her impatience to pass the information to OMEGA.

Bartholomew escorted her from his residence to the Jade Buddha, where the guests mingled for a leisurely cocktail hour. Declining a virgin mango sunrise, she opted for an alcohol-free coconut daiquiri. The creamy drink went down smoothly, as did the seared poke served for dinner.

As Danny had promised, the fish was the best thing on the menu. It had been cut into cubes, marinated in sesame-seed oil, garlic and soy sauce, and pan seared to a crunchy texture on the outside. The delicate white flakes inside were so tender they fell off Jordan's fork.

She was seated next to Felicity. The woman's mood hadn't improved much since the morning group session. Stabbing at her plate, the blonde swept a glance around the bubbling fountains and koi-filled ponds.

"Looks like our studly security director decided to skip dinner," she grumbled. "So, I notice, did our little spa director. I bet they're together, doing the naked-monkey dance."

Jordan didn't know which disgusted her more, Felicity's coarseness or the bitter taste left in her mouth by the idea TJ and Liana might be getting it on.

She wasn't jealous. You had to *care* about someone to feel jealous. But her tone held a distinctly cool note when she responded to Felicity's comment.

"Liana gave me a salt glow this afternoon. She was very professional and pleasant."

And extremely closemouthed about her employer. The most Jordan had pulled out of her was that Bartholomew preferred hot-stone therapy to deep-tissue massage.

Big surprise there. The man took his rocks seriously. His near ecstasy when he'd fondled that emerald heart earlier this evening had come close to creeping Jordan out. So had those vibrations emanating from the stone on the massive gold crucifix.

Smoke and mirrors, she told herself. It was all done with smoke and mirrors.

At least she'd gotten a good look inside the vault. She knew its layout now and had a fix on the security protecting it. She'd need special equipment to bypass the alarms and access the vault again on her own.

And, she decided reluctantly, she'd need backup. She could handle the electronics. She could also get around any sensors, including those hidden in the floors, now that she knew to look for them. But getting around the redundant on-site/off-site computer systems demanded more than one set of hands.

She added backup to her list of items to coordinate with Claire. She also wanted to hear what she'd dug up on Harry McShay, the computer mogul who'd lost his wife and daughter in a boating accident. She'd sensed more than grief behind McShay's cryptic comments this morning.

Antsy to contact Claire, she skipped dessert. She was halfway to the door when Edna Albert caught her. The widow aimed a quick look over her shoulder and dropped her voice to a raspy whisper.

"Can you come to my bungalow later?"

Jordan went still. "Why?"

Edna shot another furtive look behind her. "A few of us are getting together for a little Texas Hold 'Em. The minimum bet is a hundred, with a max of five hundred on the flop."

Relaxing, Jordan swallowed a grin. Greene

didn't allow phones or TV to disturb the tranquility of his guests. Evidently poker was on the prohibited list, as well.

"Sorry, I don't play Texas Hold 'Em."

Edna's berry-bright eyes lit up. "I'd be happy to teach you."

"Maybe some other time."

The widow puffed out her cheeks, obviously disappointed that she'd failed to reel in a new fish, and scuttled in Felicity's direction.

Once out into the night, Jordan picked up her pace and headed for her favorite bent palm. Fingering her gold hoop, she activated the transmitter.

"Diamond here. Come in, Control."

"I'm here," Claire responded. "So is Lightning. We were just about to contact you."

Ten minutes later, Jordan hammered on the locked rear door of the administrative building. Spots blinked on, dousing her in dazzling white light. Cameras whirred and aimed their eyes down at her. A hidden speaker crackled.

"Yes?"

"It's Jordan Colby. I want to talk to TJ Scott."

"Mr. Scott has gone off duty for the night."

"Where is he?" she demanded, fire in her heart.

Chapter 7

TJ sprawled against a palm. He'd shed his shirt and shoes and planted his butt in the damp sand. One leg was bent at a comfortable angle, the other stretched out to the wavelets washing like long, iridescent ribbons onto the deserted beach. Clouds scudded across the dark sky. The moon poked out every once in a while and stayed just long enough to illuminate the six-pack stuck in the sand within easy reach.

TJ was on his second beer. Two was all he ever allowed himself, on or off duty, but this was the first alcohol he'd consumed since arriving at the Tranquility Institute. He wasn't buzzed, exactly. Just loose enough that the verbal stab wounds Jordan had inflicted a couple hours ago were starting to scab over.

Not that he hadn't deserved every plunge of the dagger. He'd carry the guilt for involving her in the sting that took him down for a long, long time.

He'd never intended to let things get serious between them. Neither had Jordan. She'd told him so that Sunday afternoon in the park. Yet they clicked, right from the start. And what had begun as a casual affair got too intense, too fast.

If only the timing hadn't been so wrong...

Muttering a curse, TJ lifted the can and guzzled a long swallow. Yeasty and now warm, the beer was settling into his belly when the cell phone clipped to the waistband of his jeans began to vibrate. With another curse, he unhooked the phone and growled into the speaker.

"Scott."

"Sorry to bother you, boss. Ms. Colby is here at the security ops center. She says she has something important she needs to discuss with you."

"Put her on."

"She doesn't want to talk over the phone. She wants your present location."

What the hell...?

"Tell her I'm at the cove. She can take the stairs at the top of the bluff."

TJ snapped the phone shut. A savage sense of anticipation thrummed along his nerves. This confrontation had to come. He'd tried to force it twice. He

was ready, more than ready, for a face-to-face with
the woman he'd once burned and now suspected of
tracking him across an ocean to exact a long-over-
due revenge.

As crazy as it sounded, that was the only explanation he'd been able to come up with for Jordan's
appearance at the Tranquility Institute. The only
reason for her lies, the wet suit, the smooth way
she'd manipulated Greene into showing her his
private collection. She was after something, and TJ
suspected it was his head on a platter. This was as
good a time as any to find out how she intended to
get it there.

The call had wiped out his mellow feeling, yet he
maintained his lazy slouch against the palm. She'd
called the meeting, but they'd conduct it on his
turf—and run it by his rules.

That was the plan, anyway, until she appeared at
the top of the steep stairs. She was in the same strapless sundress she'd worn for her visit to the vault,
but she removed her high-heeled sandals and tossed
them aside before making the descent.

Barefoot, she stalked across the sand to where he
lounged under the palm. The moon popped out from
behind a cloud when she was less than a yard away,
illuminating a face tight with fury.

"Get up!"

Whatever the hell TJ had been expecting, that
snarled command wasn't it. "Come again?"

"I want you standing for this."

Curiosity beat out his determination to control the situation. He set aside the half-empty can and rolled to his bare feet.

"All right. I'm standing. Now what?"

"Now," she ground out, "I'm going to knock you on your ass."

Sheer astonishment immobilized him for the half second's edge she needed to compensate for his size and years of training. One moment he was balancing lightly on his feet, trying to figure out what had put the fire in her eyes. The next, he had a shoulder gouging into his gut and a hundred twenty pounds of female tossing him over her shoulder.

He hit with a thud that rattled his bones. Spread eagle on the sand, he sucked air back into his lungs while the wavelets tickled his soles and Jordan stood over him like an avenging angel.

He could have taken her down then. One kick, and he could have knocked her feet out from under her. Maybe. She seemed to want him to try. Before TJ took the bait, he wanted some answers.

"You going to tell me what the hell that was all about?"

"That, you bastard, was for letting me believe you were on the take."

Klaxons went off inside his head. What did she know? How had she found out?

"I told you three years ago I was set up," he said, feeling his way through this unexpected minefield. "And again when you arrived in Hawaii.

Are you saying you've suddenly decided to believe me?"

"No, *Special Agent* Scott. I'm saying my boss just advised me you took the fall deliberately and have been working undercover for the feds ever since."

Damn! TJ didn't twitch so much as a muscle, but adrenaline shot through every vein and artery in his body.

"Who," he asked, his voice low and lethal, "is your boss?"

"You don't need his name. All you need to know is that he outranks *your* boss. The way I figure it, that means you're working for me now."

"The hell you say!"

He moved then. Jordan was expecting the swift kick aimed at her ankle and dodged it neatly. She *wasn't* expecting the lightning scissor action that brought his right leg up behind the left.

The blow struck behind her knee. Knocked off balance, she went down hard. TJ rolled up and over her. Straddling her hips, he grabbed her wrists and pinned them to the sand.

Jordan ached to continue the tussle. Her blood was up. So was her fury. She knew more than one move to disable an assailant from a prone position. Unfortunately, Lightning's instructions had been succinct and to the point.

She was to cooperate. With TJ. A fellow under-cover agent. Working for the DEA.

"Okay," her new associate snarled, "let's have it. Who are you?"

"I'm the woman you know as Jordan Colby. When we're communicating on this op, you can refer to me by my code name, Diamond."

"No code names. No aliases." His hands tightened on her wrists. "Who the hell are you?"

"I'm an operative employed by a covert agency of the United States government. I have been for five years."

She could see him connecting the dots. Now he knew why her name had never popped up on the police reports. Why the media had never eviscerated her as they had him. His dawning realization that he'd been played for as much of a fool as she had gave Jordan a savage satisfaction.

"Which agency?"

"It's called OMEGA."

"I've never heard of it."

"Few individuals outside the president's immediate circle have." Impatient now, she tugged at her wrists. "Contact your controller at DEA, Scott. He'll verify that this is now a joint operation."

She could feel his reluctance to release her and his even greater reluctance to believe what she was telling him.

"My boss said to tell you the crabgrass is taking over the front yard."

The coded message passed from DEA headquarters via Lightning made no sense to Jordan, but then it didn't have to. The only one who needed to understand it was TJ.

He did. Looking like a bull that had just charged headfirst into a brick wall, he sank back on his haunches. His not inconsiderable weight landed on her belly and shoved her deeper into the wet sand.

"Well, hell!"

Resisting the impulse to squirm, Jordan huffed out an annoyed directive. "Use my code name when you talk to your controller. It will let your superior know I've established contact. As directed by *my* superior."

He sat on her for another few moments, letting his unrestrained heaviness tell her how unhappy he was with her and with the situation.

"Diamond," she said with exaggerated patience. "My code name is Diamond."

He shoved to his feet with a vicious curse. "Stay put!"

Like she was going anywhere?

Struggling upright, she wrapped her arms around her knees. Her dress was soaked and plastered to her body. Sand coated her bare back and shoulders. A few grains had worked their way into her nose and mouth. She spit out the grit and was left with only the bitter aftertaste from Lightning's startling communication.

It had taken almost twenty-four hours of solid digging to get to the truth, he'd relayed. He'd started with the officer who'd commanded the NYPD anticorruption task force. The captain stuck to his story. The task force had been watching TJ Scott for some time. They'd collected hard evidence he'd taken bribes. Then they'd screwed up on the warrant, and Scott had walked on a friggin' technicality.

It was the judge who finally admitted he'd been alerted to look for that technicality. The admission came only after Lightning had brought the pressure of the White House to bear on the judge. Even then it took more hours of sifting through bureaucratic layers to determine that the whole bust had been a setup.

As TJ had always asserted, Jordan acknowledged bitterly. He'd told her the absolute truth, dressed up to look like a lie. She hadn't believed him then. She wasn't sure she could believe him now.

She knew how bureaucracy worked. All too well. Despite the recommendations of the 9/11 Commission to streamline and centralize intelligence, the overhaul bill President Bush had signed into law had yet to break down the compartmentalization that was both the bane and the backbone of the intelligence community.

Some information *had* to be kept close-hold. The more people who were read into a program, the higher the possibility of a leak. On the other hand, the fewer who knew about clandestine operations such as this one, the greater the likelihood of crossed communications.

She had her orders. She was to apprise TJ of her

mission. He in turn would be instructed to cooperate fully with her. After what they'd put each other through three years ago, though, she suspected cooperation wouldn't equate with trust.

When he dropped down beside her a few moments later, he didn't look any more ready to forgive and forget than Jordan felt at the moment.

"All right, *Special Agent* Colby. Headquarters confirms you're on the side of justice, equality and the American way. Now suppose you tell me what the hell you're doing in the middle of my op."

"You heard about the theft of the sultana of D'han's emerald?"

He sent her a scathing look. "I may be out of the loop on some matters, but headquarters did read me in on that little incident. They also advised me Bartholomew Greene is one of the prime suspects behind the heist. In addition to being in bed with the Colombians, which is why I was sent to Hawaii in the first place."

"Have you uncovered any evidence that points to either the theft or Greene's involvement in money laundering?"

"Not yet. Have you?"

He'd slipped the blade in so smoothly it took Jordan a moment to feel the prick.

"Okay, okay. I admit it. I did some snooping around last night."

He didn't appear gratified by her grudging admission. In the dim glow of the moon, his face was all hard angles and deep creases.

"How did you bypass the security systems?"

"I used a sniffer to detect and avoid the motion sensors."

"What about the Y-beams?"

"Headquarters outfitted me with a thermal suit that contains body heat. It also," she tacked on after a moment of brittle silence, "makes me sweat like a pig. That's why my foot went out from under me on the bathroom tiles."

He angled her another look. "Did you find anything while you were poking around?"

"No."

She hated having to admit failure to another operative. Particularly *this* operative. She hadn't yet made the mental leap from thinking of him as a dirty cop.

A short, charged silence spun out while Jordan remembered the humiliation, anger and hurt she'd nursed for so long. She had to ask, had to know.

"Why did you get involved with me back in New York? Was I part of your cover? Crooked cop needs extra cash to romance his supermodel girlfriend?"

"You were never part of the sting, Red. You just…happened. For what it's worth, I never intended to take things so far between us."

"What did you intend?"

"A hot date," he replied with brutal honesty. "An even hotter weekend. That's all I had in mind when I approached you at the charity ball. I'd spent months perfecting my cover and setting myself up to take the fall. I knew the bust was coming, knew I couldn't get serious about any woman."

"So you were just filling time."

"Yeah. At first. Then…"

"Then?"

"Then things got complicated."

That was one way of describing the fire they'd ignited in each other, Jordan supposed.

"The bust wasn't supposed to net anyone except me," TJ said after a moment.

"So what went wrong?"

"A vice cop picked up a pimp I'd put the squeeze on. The pimp squealed, Vice took it to Internal Affairs and IA came down on the captain in charge of the anticorruption task force. We had planned the bust for later in the week, but with the crap about to hit the fan, the captain had to move on it. Unfortunately, he picked the same afternoon I finally got you into my bed."

"Finally?" She let out a huff of derision and disgust. "As I recall, we'd tangled between the sheets several times before that supremely regrettable session in your apartment."

"You can't regret it any more than I do."

She wasn't so sure about that. Resting her chin on her sandy knees, she let the memories of their last hour together sweep back.

As if it were yesterday, she could feel the tiny beads of sweat that had pooled at the base of TJ's spine. The rasp of his unshaven cheek against hers.

The sheer wonder of exploring his lean, muscled body with mouth and tongue and teeth. She'd never experienced anything close to that level of sensuality before. Or since.

She wouldn't have been so angry or so disgusted with herself afterward if the hunger had been purely physical. What hurt then, what *still* hurt, was the aching realization she'd come to crave his company as much as his touch.

He'd craved hers, too. The connection hadn't been all one-sided. Jordan had sensed it in the shared laughter, the verbal sparring matches, the discovery of mutual likes and avid dislikes. She had to know how he could abandon that—and her—without a backward glance.

"Why did you go undercover, TJ? Why give up twelve years on the force and let all your friends believe you'd turned?"

He didn't answer right away. Hooking his elbows over his knees, he stared out at the dark, restless sea.

"It started with an arrest I made," he said finally. "A street punk who'd robbed a convenience store. He was young, just twelve it turned out, and so stoned he couldn't remember his name. I'd busted twelve-year-olds before. Too damn many of them. But something about this one got to me. Maybe the fact that he puked all over me before I got him to the juvenile detention center."

"That would certainly endear him to me, too."

The comment drew a wry smile.

"I sort of made him my personal project after that. He didn't have anyone else who cared what happened to him. His mother had taken a hike. His father had already written him off as a dopehead and a loser. I worked with his caseworker, talked to the judge, got the kid into rehab. Social services managed to place him in a decent foster home after rehab."

Jordan had spent a number of years on her own. She knew how tough it was to climb out of the gutter and stay out. So she wasn't surprised at what came next.

"Two weeks after he got out of rehab, he OD'd."

TJ's shrug disguised the bone-deep frustration of a cop who dealt with such tragedies every day.

"The kid was just another statistic, one more throwaway, but I decided then I was tired of going after the street pushers and two-bit junkies. I wanted the big guys, the ones flooding the schools with snow and coke and meth."

"And you couldn't get to them as an NYPD narc?"

"Not the ones I wanted. Not the ones funneling the crap in by the plane- and boatload."

"So you talked to the feds."

"I talked to the feds. Then I started putting the squeeze on the pimps and pushers on my beat. Word soon got out I was looking to make more than what I could earn as a cop."

It wouldn't take long, Jordan knew. That kind of

thing was like mold. It spread to dark, dank corners almost without check.

"After I was busted for taking bribes, I let it be known I was available to the highest bidder. Surprising how many scuzz-balls wanted to hire the same cop who'd sent their friends to Rikers. Eventually, I worked my way into the inner circle of some heavy hitters. A number of them are now behind bars," he said with fierce satisfaction. "They still don't have a clue who put them there."

Three years, Jordan thought. He'd been living among scum for three years. The same kind of scum she'd once accused him of being.

"It never occurred to you to tell me you were undercover?"

"I wanted to, Red. You have no idea how badly. But I couldn't take you where I was going and I sure as hell didn't want to expose you to the kind of people I'd be dealing with."

"That's pure unadulterated crap. What you mean is that you couldn't trust me with the truth."

He slanted her a quick glance. "I'd say that worked both ways. I was a cop, a good one as far as you knew. Yet you never gave me a hint you were anything other than a supermodel turned entrepreneur."

He was right. She hadn't.

Scooping up a clump of damp sand, she crumbled it and let the grains sift through her fingers. With it went the anger at what she'd always believed was a betrayal.

"We had a chance at something," she said after a moment.

"Yes, we did."

"Too bad we screwed everything up."

"Maybe not everything. Best I recall, there were one or two things we did pretty well."

She looked up and saw his mouth curve in a grin, but didn't realize his intent until he slid a palm around her nape.

"Hold on, Scott! This is *not* a good idea. In case you've forgotten, we're on an op here."

"I haven't forgotten, Red. This is just for old time's sake."

His lips brushed hers once, twice.

Jordan knew she should pull away. Her head was whirling with everything he'd told her. And they still hadn't discussed coordinating their actions on what was now a joint mission. Neither of them had any business indulging in a maudlin bout of nostalgia, however brief.

Which didn't explain why she shifted position and angled her mouth to his. Or why heat streaked through every inch of her body.

Chapter 8

One kiss. That was all Jordan had intended. A taste of warm, wet mouth. A brief dance of tongues and teeth. Before she quite knew how it had happened, the kiss had morphed into a scene right out of *From Here To Eternity*.

She remembered slicking her hands over TJ's bare shoulders and back. And his low growl when he took her down with him onto the hard-packed sand. The next thing she knew, they were doing one heck of an imitation of Burt Lancaster and Deborah Kerr sprawled in wild abandon while waves broke over them.

"TJ!" she gasped as his mouth blazed a hot trail from her mouth to her throat. "This is insane!"

"Yeah, I know."

The surf rushed in, climbing higher onto the shore. Eddies foamed over Jordan's legs. Her dress swirled up to her thighs. Feeling ridiculous and aroused and in imminent danger of drowning, she voiced no objection when TJ scooped her up and carried her to higher ground.

Into the shadows, she noted with the minuscule corner of her brain still functioning. Hidden from anyone who might decide to stroll along the bluffs above the beach. The agent in her approved of his instinctive caution even as the female in her urged him to hurry.

Her hazy worry that the break in mouth-to-mouth contact would snap them back to sanity disappeared when TJ stooped. Balancing her on one knee, he groped for the shirt she hadn't noticed lying in the shadows and spread it into a makeshift beach blanket.

The contrast between the warm, dry cotton under her back and the cool, sleek body that covered hers jolted every one of Jordan's nerve endings. Breathing in his salty scent, she closed her eyes to the dark silhouette of the palms rustling far above them.

She wasn't as successful at closing her mind to the tiny voice inside her head. It kept whispering to her. Reminding her. This was TJ. The man she'd tumbled into love with once before. The man who'd walked away from her.

A tug on the elasticized bodice of her dress silenced the nagging whispers. The bodice came down. A moment later, the sodden skirt came up. Both ends met in a tangle around her waist.

"I'd almost forgotten how beautiful you are."

His voice was low and rough, his callused palm prickly against her skin as he traced the curve of her breasts and waist and hips.

"You're not so bad yourself."

She laid her palms against the smooth curve of skin and sinew. The feel of him tightened the muscles low in her belly. Her womb clenched and a liquid heat rushed through her veins, firing a hunger she hadn't felt in so long she'd forgotten its potency.

To hell with it. She'd sort everything out later. Right now, she wanted exactly what TJ was offering.

"We'll play this different from last time," she panted, fumbling for the snap on his jeans. "No hearts. No violins. No schmaltzy Sunday afternoons in the park. This is just sex, Scott. For old time's sake."

He went still for a moment, frowning at the way she'd thrown his words back at him. In no mood for argument or discussion, Jordan tugged down his zipper and closed her hand over the hard, hot bulge behind it. Thirty seconds later they were both naked.

"No hearts," he agreed, positioning himself between her legs. "No flowers. Just this."

Jordan's heels dug into the sand. Her thighs cradled his. When he thrust into her, she was ready.

Too ready!

Three strong, smooth strokes arched her back.

Three more brought a groan ripping from deep in her throat. Somehow, she managed to hang on until TJ's breath was as rough and as fast as hers.

Her climax shot her as high as the peaks towering above them in the darkness of the night. The aftermath floated her back down in slow, spiraling swirls.

She was still gliding when TJ fisted his hands in her hair. Bunching his thigh muscles, he thrust into her a final time.

Jordan had once read a magazine article devoted to the fine art of transitioning from bed to breakfast. The author had claimed there was no need for awkward mornings-after. No cause to feel embarrassed when rolling out of tangled sheets. All a girl needed to get through that moment of separation was a dash of wit and a dollop of panache.

Unfortunately, nothing in the article had suggested a graceful way to dust off sand, drag a soggy dress over equally soggy panties, and face the man who'd dumped you three years ago for reasons you now understood but couldn't quite forgive.

Okay, Jordan thought as she squirmed into her wet bikini briefs. All right. They'd fed the raging beast. Satisfied the hunger left over from three years ago. Now it was time to address the matter that had brought them back into each other's orbits. Folding her legs under her, she sat up and assumed as brisk an air as possible with her hair in tangles and her mouth salty with the taste of TJ's skin.

"We need to talk about Bartholomew and his operation here at the institute."

The snap on his jeans closed with a small pop. Shaking the sand from his shirt, he dragged it on.

"What have you got so far?" she asked, when he'd hunkered down beside her.

"Not a whole lot."

TJ flicked a broken piece of shell off his forearm and watched it spin into the shadows. His pulse had pretty well steadied and his brain had reengaged with his body, but he had a tough time wrapping his thoughts around either Bartholomew Greene or the Tranquility Institute. His mind was still alive with images of Jordan all taut and slick and shuddering in his arms. Filing those vivid visuals away for replay later, he channeled his thoughts to the task that had consumed him for the past three months.

"I'm pretty sure Greene's not using his guests as mules. We've had them under tight surveillance from the moment they landed at the airport and haven't uncovered any evidence they're transporting excessive amounts of cash in or out of the institute."

"*Excessive* being the operative word," Jordan murmured. "Most of the folks I've met so far could buy my business a dozen times over and barely see a dip in their bottom line."

"So could Greene's Colombian pals."

It was a vicious fact of life. The Colombian drug cartels ranked right up there with the top Fortune 500 corporations in terms of sales and beat most of them hands down when it came to profit margin. TJ knew he couldn't wipe out that margin entirely, but he sure as hell intended to put a dent in it.

The only way to get them was to go for their pressure points. Hit them where it hurt most. Despite their vast distribution and sales network, the cartels faced a serious problem when it came to converting their profits into cash. They couldn't bring the dollars they collected from their thousands of dealers into their own country. The Colombian government—with the willing and eager assistance of the United States—monitored the influx of foreign currency too closely these days. That meant the drug lords had to convert dollars to pesos.

The system was actually fairly simple. A Colombian drug trafficker or his U.S. counterpart would contact their American cohort and negotiate an exchange rate, usually thirty to forty percent below the official exchange rate. The trafficker would then arrange to have his dollars delivered to a drop-off point. The money could arrive in suitcases, shopping bags or the trunk of a car.

The American cohort would then disperse the dollars to scores of different banks. He had to keep each deposit under ten thousand dollars to avoid triggering the automatic report to law enforcement activities required on all such deposits. Once in the banking system, the money could be electronically manipulated, sent to offshore accounts and converted into pesos.

As simple as the process sounded, it still required an intake point, someone willing to accept the drug dollars and feed them into banks. The FBI, DEA and now this new agency, OMEGA, suspected Bartholomew Greene of doing just that. Proving it was turning out to be more difficult—and more dangerous—than anticipated. One DEA agent had already disappeared while attempting to penetrate Greene's organization.

Now another operative had joined TJ on the scene. Christ! Jordan Colby, undercover for some shadowy agency he'd just learned existed! How the hell was he supposed to separate the woman whose bones he'd just jumped from the agent he'd been instructed to cooperate with?

"We're talking millions of dollars collected from thousands of pushers," he growled, making the attempt. "If Greene's accepting that kind of cash, laundering it through a series of banks and converting it to pesos for his South American friends, it has to funnel in somewhere."

"An isolated tropical resort surrounded by enough security to protect the U.S. national gold reserves seems like a pretty good place to make the drop."

"You'd think. As I said, we've monitored everyone arriving and departing the institute. If any of the guests acted as a courier, I haven't found evidence of it yet."

"What about McShay?"

"The Silicon Valley king? We scrubbed him with

a wire brush. He came up clean." TJ's glance sharpened on the woman next to him. "Why? Did he say something that made you suspicious?"

Her face was little more than a pale blur, but he could hear the frown in her voice.

"It wasn't so much what he said, but how he said it. McShay gave me the distinct impression he owed Bartholomew his soul."

"He does. From all reports, Greene pulled the man back from the brink of suicide."

Despite his suspicions about the psychotherapist, TJ had to admit the man seemed to know his business. The files included case after case of people claiming Bartholomew had helped them come to grips with everything from eating disorders to the death of a loved one.

"I still want to talk to McShay," Jordan said. "Maybe I can get him to open up."

Swallowing a bone-deep reluctance to let an outsider jump into the middle of his op, TJ shrugged. "Go for it."

"I assume you've also scrubbed the institute's employees? Duncan Myers? Liana Wu? Danny the driver?"

"We're pretty sure Myers is skimming corporate profits, but we haven't been able to link him to drug money. Danny is clean. So is Wu."

A mental image of the delectable spa director formed in TJ's mind. Liana had dropped several hints that she wanted to get together and discuss more spa security. He'd been interested—and not just for the information he might elicit about Greene—but had sidestepped her subtle invitations to get up close and personal.

James Bond could tumble suspects into bed. The DEA tended to frown on that sort of thing. TJ had a feeling his bosses wouldn't be happy knowing he'd tumbled an undercover operative into the sand, either.

Now that he was thinking with his head instead of his heart, he wasn't particularly thrilled about it himself. He couldn't remember the last time he'd let down his guard like that. Anyone could have strolled across the beach and put a gun to his head. He would have died happy at that point. The problem was, Jordan might well have died with him.

Cursing his brief descent into insanity, TJ made a swift, silent vow not to put her at risk again. That glorious session in the sand might have healed some old hurts and opened new areas for exploration, but they couldn't sink into that kind of near oblivion again. Not here. Not until they'd nailed Bartholomew Greene and his accomplices.

Afterward...

No, better not go there. He had too much at stake right here, right now, to indulge in fantasies about the unforeseeable future.

"What about the local businesses who supply goods and services to the institute?" Jordan wanted to know. "Someone could be hauling in truckloads of dollars along with tons of pineapples and kiwi. Or hauling it out for distribution to various banks on the island."

"We've worked the locals. We've also worked the banks here on Kauai. There aren't enough of them to absorb the kind of deposits we're talking about without hitting the ten-thousand-dollar trigger."

"So the deposits have to be going into banks on the mainland."

"That's our best guess."

"But Greene spends most of his time in Hawaii."

"I know," he said dryly. "That's why I'm here."

"'Scuse me?"

It took a moment to click. "Sorry. That's why we're here."

Accepting the correction with a nod, she pursed her lips in concentration. An aftershock jolted through TJ when he remembered how those lips had been all over him just moments ago.

Dammit! He had to get that session in the sand out of his head. Get *everything* out of his head but Greene and friends. One friend in particular had his special interest.

"You know Greene's primary emerald supplier arrives tomorrow?"

"Myers told me," Jordan replied. "Alejandro Garcia. My people are checking him out."

TJ hoped her people could dig up more on Garcia than his had. Not even the undercover operative who'd infiltrated the mine at Muzo had been able to tag the slick and very successful salesman as a go-between.

"Myers has set me up to meet with Garcia and associates," Jordan said. "He thinks he can cut a special deal for me and the institute."

"Where's the meeting to take place?"

"I don't know. I'm assuming the conference room in the main corporate offices."

"The meeting might start there. If Greene and Garcia decide to conduct any private business, they'll do it away from the security cameras in the conference area."

"Have you bugged every private alcove and office?"

"What do you think?"

"I don't know. That's why I'm asking."

"I can't get a wiretap or install unauthorized listening devices without a warrant, and I can't obtain a warrant until I convince a judge there's probable cause. Right now, I'm depending on the security system already in place to collect info."

Jordan pooched her lips again. "I'll see what I can get out of this Garcia."

"Just stay where I can keep you on the monitors. This guy's a slick operator."

"I don't need big brother watching me. I'll signal you if I require assistance."

"How?"

"This is how."

Hooking back her tangled hair, she flicked the gold hoop in her ear.

"The transmitter inside this baby emits a signal that can't be intercepted or interpreted except at OMEGA. My controller can relay any SOSs to you via your cell phone or the phones at your security operations center."

Incredulous, TJ squinted at the gold hoop. "You've got that kind of technology packed in there?"

"Yep."

"I need to talk to our techies," he muttered.

"You do that. In the meantime, I'll meet with Garcia, Myers and, if he joins the party, Greene. I also want to talk to McShay. Why don't we get together tomorrow afternoon and compare notes."

TJ didn't particularly care for the way she'd relegated him to the sidelines but accepted her suggestion with a shrug. He also had a few things that needed doing between now and the scheduled arrival of the Colombians. None of them involved Jordan.

Or so he thought until she pushed to her feet, plucked at her dress to untangle the folds and shook off a shower of sand. The moon put out just enough glow to silhouette her legs against the wet, almost transparent fabric.

The memory of those slim thighs and calves wrapped around him such a short time ago hit TJ like a power jab to the jaw. Smothering a curse, he scooped up the remnants of his six-pack and reordered his priorities. The first thing on his agenda had to be a long, cold shower.

Chapter 9

Jordan woke the next morning primed for her meeting with Alejandro Garcia. When she tilted the plantation shutters to let in the dazzling light, anticipation hummed along her nerves and stirred up her senses.

The hibiscus crowding the lanai smelled sweeter, stronger. The ocean chanted a surging rhythm. Refusing to dwell on how much of her supercharged energy stemmed from that incredible, insane session with TJ last night, she washed, dragged a brush through her hair, slapped on a minimum of makeup and dressed.

Thank God for the resort's elegant boutiques and well-stocked gift shops! She'd augmented the limited wardrobe she'd packed into the carryall with strategic purchases, one of which had bitten the dust last night. The white-on-white sundress sat in a plastic laundry sack, crying for cleaning. The gauzy shorts and turquoise halter top would work for the morning group session, but not the meeting with the Colombians. She settled for freshly laundered linen slacks and a sleeveless silk blouse in a soft peach that brought out the highlights in her deep auburn hair. Draping a multistrand link belt with hundreds of dangling charms around her hips, she reached for the finishing touch.

The emerald teardrop felt cool when she picked it up, warm when it nestled against her skin. She stood still for a moment, frowning at the odd sensation that seemed to emanate from the stone. Not a vibration, exactly. Not an out-and-out quiver. Just a small tremor, as if it was absorbing her energy.

"Don't get crazy, Colby. Remember, it's a trick."

With that stern admonition, she left her cottage and joined the guests who'd gathered for the breakfast buffet at the Jade Buddha. Harry McShay wasn't among them, Jordan saw in a quick sweep of the tables. Swallowing her disappointment, she followed the hostess past ice sculptures, juice fountains and a waffle station sporting a wicked array of toppings to a table set beside the three-tiered pool.

"Just coffee," she told the waiter before helping herself to slices of fresh pineapple and a toasted bagel. The waffles were screaming her name, but old habits died hard. She'd added a thin spread of low-fat cream cheese to one half of the bagel and was ready to chow down when TJ appeared.

Her hand halted halfway to her mouth. He looked like she felt, she thought as her stomach performed a ridiculous little flip-flop. Relaxed on the outside, yet moving with a stride that suggested a coiled energy on the inside. He also looked so good she had to remind herself to breathe.

His hair was slick and dark from his shower. His knit shirt clung to his powerful shoulders and torso. Remembering the feel of that body pressing hers into the sand, Jordan gulped.

"Morning, Red."

Pulling out a chair, he joined her. The tangy lime scent of his aftershave drifted across the table as he helped himself to the other half of her bagel and smothered it with a thick layer of cream cheese.

"Alejandro Garcia and friends took the red-eye shuttle from Bogotá via Miami and LAX. They arrive at the Kauai airport at nine-twenty."

"I know. I got word late last night."

Claire had passed her the news when Jordan had contacted OMEGA to confirm she'd established liaison with TJ. She hadn't specified just how close a liaison. Headquarters didn't need such minor details.

"Do you also know Harry McShay checked out of the institute?" TJ asked as he crunched into the toasted bagel.

"No! When?"

"A half hour ago. Danny's driving him to the airport as we speak."

Dammit! She should have tracked the man down last night. She *would* have, if she hadn't become otherwise occupied. That's what came of giving in to old hurts and new hungers. Thoroughly disgusted with herself, Jordan reached for her coffee cup.

"McShay booked a first-class seat on the turnaround of the same flight bringing in Garcia and company," TJ said, his voice low. "They'll pass each other at the gate."

The quiet announcement sent her cup clattering back onto the saucer. Her thoughts racing, Jordan darted a quick look across the table.

"The timing could be coincidental."

"McShay was scheduled to remain at the institute for another week."

"Maybe he got called back to the mainland on business."

"If so, the call didn't come through the central switchboard."

Her mind scrambled, trying to fit the pieces together. "We need to get him under surveillance."

"It's done."

"Not just at the Kauai airport. You said Garcia and pals flew via Miami and Los Angeles. They could have left something for McShay with one of the flight attendants. Or at the L.A. airport. A key, an envelope, a map, anything. We need someone on the man from the moment he deplanes."

"It's done, Jordan."

She sat back, eyeing him with grudging respect. "Sounds like you've been busy. Anything left for me to do?"

"You've got group this morning, right? Feel out the other guests, see if they know anything about McShay's abrupt departure. And get me on that net you told me about last night. I want to test the reception before you waltz into your meeting with Garcia."

Jordan tipped him a mock salute. "Yes, sir. Right away, sir. Anything else, sir?"

"Not at the moment." His grin slipped out, quick and slashing and all TJ. "Something might come to me later."

Scarfing down the rest of her bagel, he pushed back his chair.

Jordan sensed a difference the moment she walked into the large, airy room at the Meditation Center.

Yesterday the group members had exhibited friendly curiosity. Today, the atmosphere felt considerably less convivial. Felicity paced the room with a restlessness that matched her disgruntled expression. Edna slouched in her chair, looking querulous. The poker game must have run late, Jordan thought, eyeing the tired slump to the widow's shoulders.

Even Davy seemed more withdrawn, if that was possible. The boy hunched in his chair, legs tucked under him, and worked his Game Boy with both thumbs. His sandy hair fell forward over his forehead and his breath came in small, quick wheezes.

"Hi, Davy. What are you playing?"

He didn't glance up. "Yu-Gi-Oh TrailMaster."

"Are you winning?"

"I always win." Another wheeze whistled up from his thin chest. "This is a dumb little kid's game, but my mom won't let me buy Ice Nine."

Concerned by his uneven breathing, Jordan hesitated by his side. "You feeling okay?"

His shoulders drew up around his ears. He seemed to want to fold in on himself and refused to meet her eyes.

"Ignore him," Felicity said with sharp impatience. "He's just in one of his bratty moods because he's stuck here at the institute with a bunch of losers instead of being in school with other kids."

Edna took exception to her sweeping indictment. "Speak for yourself, young lady. I for one am no loser. I cleaned up last night. Just ask Harry how much he lost on that last flop."

"Harry McShay?" Jordan dropped the name casually. "Did he join your poker game?"

"Sure did. Bet a bundle on a full house and lost it to my four eights."

"Maybe that's why he left so early this morning. You cleaned him out."

Edna's eyes widened. "Harry's gone?"

"Didn't he mention leaving to you last night?"

"No."

Jordan wanted to dig deeper but just then Davy erupted into a fit of coughing. His Game Boy dropped to the floor. His thin chest heaved in and out. Between the hacking coughs, he gasped for breath.

"Omigod!" Felicity's impatience morphed into alarm. "He's having one of his attacks. Where's Bartholomew?" She threw a worried glance around the room, as if she could conjure the absent psychotherapist out of thin air. "Why the hell isn't he here?"

Jordan knew nothing about asthma attacks and had no idea what triggered this one. She had to do something, though, and fast. The boy's face was now brick red and his breath came in strangled gasps. She spun around and spotted a fire alarm on the wall beside Edna's chair.

"Pull that fire alarm! We need some help here."

Edna shot off her chair as if fired from a cannon and yanked the white lever. A thin, pulsating wail filled the air as Jordan dropped to her knees beside the panting boy.

"Do you have your medicine with you? Davy! Listen to me! Do you have some medicine on you?"

The boy was bent almost double, coughing and wheezing. His movements jerky, he dragged a plastic inhaler from his pocket, shook it a few times and jammed it in his mouth. His desperate pumping produced nothing but air.

"No...albuterol. Forgot...to change...canister."
Hell!

"Someone find his mother," Jordan shouted over
the wail of the siren. "Now!"

One of the men took off at a run. The other group
members crowded around, helpless, while Davy's
tear-filled eyes pleaded with Jordan to do something, anything. She tried to think, tried to shut her
mind to the screaming siren and the boy's wheezing.

"Meditation!" Felicity pressed forward, wanting
to help. "We can try meditation! Bartholomew's
been working with Davy on the techniques."

The blonde slapped a hand to the emerald pinned
to her right shoulder and began a low, discordant
chant. The others jumped on her suggestion. Hands
dug in pockets and produced emeralds. Eyes shut
tight. Murmurs rose to compete with the wail of the
fire alarm and Davy's heartbreaking pants.

Jordan didn't see any other option. Until help
arrived, all she could do was try to calm the boy and,
hopefully, ease the panic restricting his air passages.

She searched her mind for the ritual steps Bartholomew had taken the group through yesterday.
The stone! First he'd had them grasp their healing
stones.

"Davy! Do you have your emerald?"

"Right...here."

His motions spastic, he pointed to his shirt
pocket. Jordan fished out his emerald and pressed
it into his palm.

"Okay. Close your eyes! Come on, close them."

What came next? What the *hell* had come next?

"Take a deep…"

She bit that back. No way the kid could pull a deep breath into his starved lungs.

"Think about the world around you." She kept her voice as low and calm as she could and still be heard over the pulsing siren. "Pretend you're taking a walk on the beach. Can you hear the waves? See them rolling in? Washing over the sand? Retreating? They're so smooth. So green and sparkling. Do you see them, Davy? Here they come again. In and out. In and out."

Smoke and mirrors. Oh, God, please don't let this all be smoke and mirrors!

Jordan closed her fist around the emerald teardrop dangling between her breasts. The pointed tip dug into her palm as she forced herself to continue the rhythmic chant.

"Walk along the beach with me, Davy. Squeeze the sand between your toes. Feel the sun warm your face. Here comes another wave. There's another one right behind it. In, out. In, out."

Felicity crouched beside them, her face twisting with fear and hope. "He's breathing easier!"

If he was, Jordan couldn't tell it. His wheezing ripped her heart into small pieces.

"Do you feel the breeze, Davy? The cool, wet surf? The waves swirling around your ankles? Here comes another one. In, out. In, out."

She had no idea how long she knelt beside the boy. Not more than a few minutes, although it felt like hours before a hand gripped her shoulder.

"Okay, Red. I've got his medicine. I'll take it from here."

Scooting over, Jordan yielded her place to TJ's solid reassuring bulk. She'd never been so glad to see anyone in her life!

He hunkered down in front of the boy, ripped open a plastic prescription bag and replaced the empty canister in the inhaler with a fresh one. "Here you go, Dave. Breathe in. Again. Atta way, kid."

His eyes wild above the inhaler, Davy puffed in the life-saving albuterol.

TJ gauged his intake. "Okay, that's good. Let the medicine work. Someone shut off that alarm!"

Edna scuttled to the box again and shoved up the lever. The screeching died a few seconds later, leaving only Davy's awful gasping to fill the void.

Slowly the helpless wheezing gave way to pants, then to long, shuddering breaths. Jordan sank back on her heels and mouthed a silent prayer of thanks.

"Davy!"

Patricia Helms flew through the door at that moment, panic etched in every line of her body. Bartholomew charged in at her heels. Crouching down he checked his patient's pulse and probed the situation.

"Are you all right, David?"

"Yes…sir."

The panic had disappeared and left a small, shaken boy in its wake.

"Sounds like this was a bad one."

"It was."

"Did you practice the relaxation techniques I taught you when you felt the attack coming on?"

Looking guilty, Davy fidgeted in his seat. "I was playing Yu-Gi-Oh. I sorta didn't know it was coming until I started coughing."

Bartholomew's gaze dropped to the object clenched in his patient's fist. "But you remembered your healing stone. Good boy!"

"I forgot that, too," the child confessed. "But Jordan remembered. She made me hold it. I had it in my hand the whole time she walked on the beach with me."

"You walked on the beach?"

"In my head. We walked together in my head. Jordan was right there, talking to me the whole time. She got me to think about other stuff, just like you do in group."

Greene pivoted, surprise and delight stamped on his face. "How wonderful! A new disciple."

Patricia Helms expressed her appreciation more directly. Throwing her arms around Jordan, she burst into sobs. "Thank you!"

"You're welcome."

Jordan patted Patricia's thin, shaking back. Only now did she appreciate the terror the parent of an asthmatic child must live with every day. Davy's attack had certainly scared the crap out of *her*.

She'd also gained a far deeper appreciation of the desperation that brought people to Bartholomew Greene. She wasn't ready to admit a rock had anything to do with the few extra moments she'd bought Davy, but she couldn't dismiss the notion, either. Particularly since she'd gouged a good-size hole in her own palm with her borrowed emerald.

"You should really thank TJ," she said, patting Patricia's back. "He got here with Davy's medicine just in time."

TJ also received a fierce hug.

"Thank you. For getting here so quickly *and* for suggesting I leave a spare canister of albuterol at the security center. How did you know Davy needed it?"

"We don't monitor the Meditation Center during therapy sessions, but we do have security cameras in place. They kicked on when the fire alarm activated."

"I pulled the fire alarm," Edna put in, edging into the circle.

"Sure," Felicity scoffed. Now that the crisis had passed, she was looking and sounding restless again. "After Jordan told you to."

"I swear I don't know why you always have to be such a pain in the tuchas. You're almost as bad as my daughters."

TJ stepped in to play peacemaker. "You did good, Ms. Albert. When the alarm went off, I saw what was happening and hotfooted it over here."

Hotfooted it, hell! TJ had taken one look at the

drama playing out on the screen, grabbed the kid's medicine and made the two-hundred-or-so-yard dash in Olympic record time. His heart was still pumping.

Bartholomew's was too, he guessed, but you couldn't tell it from the therapist's beaming smile. "I trusted my instincts when I hired you. You've more than proved them right."

Hardly, TJ thought sardonically. Fighting to keep his expression neutral, he said nothing as Greene gave his shoulder a squeeze and turned to Jordan.

"I trusted my instincts with you, too." Reaching out, he gathered her hands in his. "Now you need to trust yours."

Frowning, she looked down at their joined hands. Her hair fell forward in a smooth auburn sweep, hiding her face. When she raised her head again, her glance cut to TJ for·a fraction of a second.

"Maybe I do."

The image of TJ kneeling in front of Davy stayed with Jordan through what remained of the shortened group session. The small crisis had seemed to have bonded her and Scott in a very different way from their tussle in the sand last night. That was pure sex. Amazing sex, granted, but still just a physical reaction resulting from the clash of two strong-willed people, both hauling baggage.

Jordan had awakened this morning convinced she'd finally dumped the residual anger and hurt left over from three years ago. She was also convinced she and TJ could team up for this mission and go their separate ways afterward. No harm, no foul, no hard feelings on either side.

The incident with Davy put a dent in that confidence. Jordan admired TJ's foresight in obtaining a backup supply of medicine from the boy's mom almost as much as the calm he'd exhibited after arriving on the scene. He'd been so good with the boy, so gentle. As he had been with her, Jordan remembered, brushing her thumb over her mottled bruise.

Irritated by the confused and wholly contradictory feelings the man stirred in her, she shoved her hand in her pocket. She had other things that needed thinking about. Like McShay's sudden departure and the imminent arrival of Alejandro Garcia.

Jordan had contacted Claire and advised her that TJ's people had McShay under surveillance. She'd also received a thorough background brief on Garcia. She was ready, more than ready, for a face-to-face with the Colombians.

Or so she thought, until she walked into the conference room just before noon and recognized Garcia's associate.

Chapter 10

When Jordan spotted the taller of the two men who entered the conference room, her heart leapfrogged from her chest to her throat.

Oh, hell!

She blew out a breath, trying to steady herself, while Bartholomew greeted his business associate. "Alejandro! So glad to have you back at the Tranquility Institute."

Using the hearty exchange of greetings as cover, Jordan took a half step to the side. A leafy dieffenbachia shadowed her as she raised her hand to scratch the tip of her nose with a polished oval nail. Her open palm hid the slight movement of her lips.

"Control, we have a problem."

The sensitive transmitter in the gold hoop picked up her low murmur. Claire's reply floated into her ear an instant later. Smothered by the thick sweep of Jordan's hair, it was inaudible to anyone but her.

"What kind of problem, Diamond?"

"I know the man with Garcia."

Claire's response was instant and expected. "Do you need backup?"

Her mind churning, Jordan assessed the situation. Claire had TJ on the other net. He could ride to the rescue when and if she gave the signal.

"Not yet."

That's all she had time for. Greene, Duncan Myers and the two new arrivals had completed their ritual of hearty handshakes and backslaps. The taller of the two slid his hands in his pockets, looking casual and relaxed.

Too relaxed, Jordan thought grimly as she moved away from the shadow of the dieffenbachia and strolled forward. She aimed her smile at Alejandro Garcia, but her peripheral vision stayed locked on the man who'd accompanied him.

He didn't blink. Didn't say a word. If not for the slight narrowing of his eyes, she might have believed he hadn't recognized her. Taking her cue from him, she gave no indication she knew him as Bartholomew grasped her elbow and drew her into the all-male circle.

"Jordan, this is my friend and longtime business

associate. Alejandro Garcia, may I present Jordan Colby, a new friend and, hopefully, also a new business associate."

Garcia was short and rotund, with wavy black hair. The emerald business must be doing well, Jordan thought as she extended her hand. His pinstriped suite was Brioni, his shoes Bally, and the glittering stone in his pinkie ring looked like Colombian prime.

"It is a pleasure to meet you, Ms. Colby. I have seen your pictures in many magazines. May I say you are even more beautiful in person than in print?"

"You may, indeed, Mr. Garcia."

"Since it is my hope that we, too, shall become business associates, you must call me Alejandro."

Smiling, she nodded to the hard-sided case he'd rolled in with him. "I would say our future relationship depends a great deal on what's in that case."

"Ah, the contents will truly astound you." His lips curled, revealing blindingly white teeth. "And you, Bartholomew. I've brought something I know you will wish to add to your private collection."

The therapist's eyes lit up. "You have?"

"I have. I'll show you in a moment. First let me introduce the man who makes me feel so secure traveling with my precious stone. Ms. Colby, Bartholomew, Duncan…this is Colonel Luis Esteban."

Jordan half expected to hear a hiss of indrawn breath in her ear. She should have known better. Claire was too well trained to react to the name of her handsome, debonair, sometime lover.

Jordan had met the Latin American only once, at a Washington cocktail party. Esteban had lifted Jordan's hand to his mustached lips with old-world charm and murmured that American women were truly among the most beautiful. Since he turned to the woman on his arm and included her in the compliment, a smiling Claire had agreed.

Looking into his dark eyes, Jordan had to admit he was as jaw-droppingly gorgeous in the bright light of a Hawaiian afternoon as he'd appeared at that cocktail party. Curling black hair, bronzed skin and a killer smile, all wrapped up in six-two of solid male.

"Luis was chief of the Cartozan Special Forces before his retirement from the military," Garcia explained. "He then worked for the president of Mexico as a private consultant until we lured him away to handle security for our courier and distribution system."

Claire had to be wondering whether Esteban had gone over to the enemy. Jordan was wondering the same thing. Her mind jumped with the possibility she might be working with two cops who'd gone bad—at least as far as the rest of the world was concerned.

With the same smiling charm he'd demonstrated the night they'd met, Esteban lifted Jordan's hand to his lips. His cloud-soft mustache tickled her skin.

"It's a pleasure to meet you, Ms. Colby. I, too, have seen your picture in many magazines. And I very much admire your elegant eyeglasses. My sister-in-law reads the newspaper through a pair with your diamond logo."

"If Alejandro and I can negotiate a satisfactory price, perhaps she'll switch to a pair with a butterfly made of emeralds from his mine."

"Perhaps she will."

Garcia took that as a signal to get down to business. Declining Bartholomew's offer of refreshments, the wholesaler collapsed the telescoping handle on his wheeled aluminum sample case and lifted it onto the conference table. Jordan made a show of not watching too closely while he spun the combination locks. She could get into the case easily enough later if she needed to.

The front opened, revealing a nest of twelve or fifteen trays. Jordan had dealt with enough diamond sales reps to know the contents of those trays would be sorted by color, clarity, cut and carat weight—the all-important four Cs of the gem world.

"Duncan faxed me a copy of your proposal," Garcia said. "Your designs call for stones a half carat or less in weight, graded VVS1 in clarity. I brought a representative sampling for you to examine."

Still trying to factor in Esteban's unexpected appearance into her mental equation, Jordan forced her attention to the tray Garcia slid out.

"These stones range from light to good in color."

The loose gems winked up at Jordan from their

velvet nest. Unlike diamonds, hue and tone were the most important factors in evaluating colored gemstones. This was especially true of emeralds. Bright, rich, intense greens commanded higher prices than light or very dark tones.

Sliding a flat wooden case out of her shoulder bag, she extracted a folding jeweler's loupe and a set of tweezers. She wasn't a certified gemologist, but she'd been in the business long enough to recognize quality when she saw it.

These emeralds were definitely top quality. Their cuts were smooth, their color rich, and their inclusions appeared only under the ten-power magnification.

Jordan knew better than to appear overly impressed. She'd worked up those proposals as a means to get her foot in the door at the institute. Greene, Myers and Garcia didn't know that, however. They'd expect her to employ tough negotiating skills.

"These might do for the less expensive lines of eyewear I'm proposing. I want a more symmetrical cut and richer color for the higher-end products."

"I see you are a woman of discerning taste," Garcia said unctuously. He slid out another tray. "Perhaps these will meet your standards. They range in color from very good to exceptional, and from medium to medium dark in tone."

The loose gems gleamed like cats' eyes peering through a dark night. Jordan selected a pear-shaped stone with the tweezers and squinted at it through the loupe. The cuts were symmetrical and the surfaces reflected the light evenly. The intense color blew her away.

"This is closer to what I had in mind," she said in a cool tone that suggested she'd seen better. "What are we talking about in terms of price per carat?"

Garcia put a pudgy finger to his lips, as if performing mental calculations. The emerald in his pinkie ring caught the light. The stone was almost as eye-catching as the monster that marked the epicenter of Bartholomew Greene's empire in the wall map behind him.

"For that size and quality," he said after a moment, "we would normally ask no less than two hundred U.S. dollars per carat weight. Since you will be marketing your products through our dear friend, Bartholomew, we can go one-eighty."

That was well below market and less than Jordan had anticipated, even from a *dear friend* of Bartholomew Greene's.

"I would hope you can do better than that," she countered, playing the game. "Another source gave me an estimate of one-fifty."

"For VVS1 stones of this color and intensity! Surely not."

"They're Thai emeralds," she admitted with a shrug. "I would prefer Colombian, but only if I can make a satisfactory profit."

"One-fifty." Garcia tapped his lips again. "I must consult my superiors before I can agree to such a price. It is late, but I may be able to reach them. Duncan, may I use your office?"

"Of course."

Bartholomew countered with a suggestion. "Perhaps you should show me what else you've brought first? We may need to do some haggling, too."

"For this, my friend, I think you will most definitely wish to haggle."

Sliding out another, deeper tray, Garcia lifted out a chunk of black graphite. Embedded in the graphite was a ten-inch shaft of green beryl. Bartholomew started salivating almost before he got his hands around the magnificent uncut emerald.

"My God! Where was this found?"

"The north vein of number-twelve shaft."

His face filled with reverence, Greene turned the piece to examine it from all angles. "I thought that vein had played out."

"We had thought so, too, until we caught one of the miners attempting to smuggle this piece out. The man is no longer employed at the Muzo mine."

Jordan guessed he was no longer employed *anywhere*. In fact, she'd lay odds he was buried at the bottom of another shaft.

Interesting that Bartholomew knew so much about Muzo operations. She'd get Claire to run his passport, see when he'd made his last visit to the source of his favorite stones.

"What are you asking for this?" Bartholomew wanted to know, tilting the piece to catch the light.

"Perhaps we should conduct our negotiations in your office," Garcia suggested. "We don't need to bore Ms. Colby or Colonel Esteban with our haggling." His white teeth flashed in a deprecating smile as he closed his case and spun the combination lock.

"Yes, yes, of course." Bartholomew couldn't scurry out of the conference room fast enough. Holding the rough emerald before him like a beacon, he threw an apology over his shoulder.

"Please excuse us, Jordan, Luis. Perhaps you'd like to have some refreshments. Or enjoy the view from the veranda. It's quite spectacular."

When the door swished shut behind the other three men, silence settled over the conference room. Esteban glanced at Jordan, his expression unreadable, before shifting his gaze to the red, unwinking eye of the security camera above her head.

"I should like to enjoy the view from this veranda Bartholomew speaks of. Will you join me?"

"Diamond!"

Claire's urgent whisper filled her ear, blanketed by the sweep of her hair. "Your friend Scott says to stay inside the conference room, where he can keep you on the monitors."

Jordan weighed TJ's instruction against Esteban's obvious desire to get outside, away from the cameras and their sensitive microphones. He had something he wanted to discuss in private and Jordan had to find out what the Cartozan was doing here.

"Shall we go outside?" the colonel asked politely. "I believe this door leads out onto the veranda."

He worked the lever and slid the glass panel open. With a little bow, he gestured Jordan onto the lanai. She stepped onto the windswept deck, almost certain she was doing the right thing.

Once outside, Esteban surveyed the area with a quick glance. Whatever he saw must have satisfied him. Turning back to Jordan, he palmed a silver cigarette case from his suit pocket.

"Do you mind if I smoke?"

"No."

"These are hand rolled for me in Cuba. They're quite mild. Would you care to try one?"

Declining one of the thin black cigarillos, she leaned an elbow on the railing and waited while he lit up. The stiff ocean breeze blew the stream of smoke out to sea.

"So, Jordan, we meet again."

"So we do."

"Are you truly here to conduct business with Bartholomew Greene?"

"Why else would I be here?"

"Why else, indeed?"

He blew another thin stream and tapped a manicured nail on his silver cigarette case a time or two before setting it squarely on the railing.

"You may speak freely. We won't be overheard."

Jordan eyed the slim case, wondering if it emitted a signal strong enough to jam the transmitter in her earring. If so, Claire would *not* be happy. Nor would TJ.

"You first," she said to Esteban. "Are you really working for the Colombians?"

"I am."

"Why?"

"I have my reasons for infiltrating their organization." He flicked an ash over the railing. "You will have to trust me that they are very much in concert with yours."

"What makes you think I'm trying to infiltrate anything?"

"You've established contact with Bartholomew Greene. You're now dealing with Garcia. You wish to discover if it is more than the buying and selling of emeralds from the Muzo mine that links them. So do I."

Jordan wanted to believe him. According to the OMEGA rumor mill, Claire Cantwell and this sexy Latin had quite a history.

"Turn that off," she said, jerking her chin at the silver case.

Shrugging, he slid a finger along the edge of the case. Jordan hooked her hair behind her ear and spoke clearly enough to be heard over the wind and restless waves.

"This is Diamond. Come in, Control."

Esteban's glance skimmed from her face to her hands, searching for the hidden transmitter. Jordan didn't clue him in.

"Go ahead, Diamond."

"Did you copy that?"

"Copy what? We've experienced some static. The airwaves just cleared."

"Colonel Esteban informed me he's deliberately infiltrated the Colombian emerald cartel."

There was a short, sharp silence. "Did he say why?"

"No. Run him, Cyrene. Now. I'll stand by."

At the mention of the code name, Esteban's eyes narrowed. "Are you speaking with Claire?"

"I'm speaking with my controller."

"How?"

With a sense of déjà vu, Jordan tapped the gold hoop with a nail. She'd played the same scene with TJ only last night. Frowning, Esteban tossed his cigarillo over the railing and moved in for a closer look.

"I wish to speak with her."

"Sorry, this is a restricted net. Anything you want to say to Cyrene, you say through me."

Jordan felt a flicker of unease as the colonel's face hardened. She glanced over the rail at the long drop to the churning sea below. Danny's tale about the ancient Hawaiians tossing folks off Ma'aona Peak onto the wave-swept rocks flashed into her head.

She coiled her muscles, fully prepared to take

the sinewy colonel down if necessary. He read the warning in her eyes and held up both palms.

"If you are as skilled as Claire, I know better than to risk my manhood by forcing matters. I shall, as you instruct, speak through you."

He spread his legs, making himself even more vulnerable to a knee to the groin, and braced his hands on either side of Jordan's waist. His breath brushing her cheek, he spoke directly into her earring.

"Buenos días, mi amor."

Jordan waited several beats, the small of her back pressed into the rail. "Did you, er, copy that, Control?"

"Yes."

The terse response sounded so un-Claire-like Jordan blinked.

"Tell Colonel Esteban to stand by," her controller rapped out. "I'm running him now."

Jordan dutifully relayed the message, although the Cartozan was close enough now to pick up the transmission himself.

"She says to stand by."

"Yes, I heard. What extraordinary clarity," he commented. "And what pleasure it gives me to hear your voice again, *querida.* We've been too long apart this time."

His breath was rich with the scent of tobacco, his mustache silky where it tickled Jordan's cheek. She'd only encountered one other man who packed so much raw masculinity into his frame.

As if the mere thought had the power to make TJ materialize, he came through the open door seconds later, moving with lethal speed and silence. Jordan glimpsed him over Esteban's broad shoulder. She also glimpsed murder in TJ's gunmetal-gray eyes.

Oh, Lord! Like Claire, he must have missed some of the transmission. Jordan had no idea how much he'd heard or hadn't heard.

"TJ, wait!"

Her shout jolted Esteban into action. In a lightning move, the colonel whipped a hand inside his suit coat, whirled around and aimed the muzzle of a blue-steel Glock at TJ's heart.

Chapter 11

"It's okay! Luis, it's okay!"

Her heart hammering, Jordan shoved away from the railing and leaped between the two men. The action precipitated a curse from Esteban and a snarl from TJ.

Snagging her wrist, TJ shoved her behind him and thrust out an arm to keep her there. *She* grabbed a fistful of his shirt to keep him from lunging for the colonel.

"Stand down! Both of you!"

The two men remained squared off, taking each other's measure, anticipating the other's next move. Fearing the imminent outbreak of hostilities, Jordan thumped TJ between the shoulder blades.

"Hey! Stand down, Scott! You, too, Esteban."

The colonel lowered the gun slowly. "Who is this man, Jordan?"

TJ answered for himself. "The name's Scott. Thomas Scott."

Something flickered in the colonel's dark eyes. "So you are Scott. I have heard of you."

Through Claire? Jordan wondered. Or through the underworld network? With her heart still pounding under the peach silk of her blouse, she stepped around her living shield.

"Perhaps I should introduce myself." Thumbing the safety on his Glock, Esteban slid it back into his underarm holster. "I am—"

"Colonel Luis Esteban," TJ rapped out, never taking his eyes off the man. "Former chief of the Cartozan Special Forces and now a hired gun for the Colombians. I had you on-screen in the conference room."

"Yes, I saw the cameras." The colonel spoke slowly, carefully. "Did you mount hidden cameras or listening devices out on this deck, as well, or may we speak freely?"

"That depends on what you want to talk about."

"Maria Fuentes."

A sudden stillness gripped TJ. The air around Jordan seemed to crackle with a new tension, one that raised the fine hairs on her arms.

"How did you know Maria?"

"May we speak freely?" Esteban repeated.

"Yes. Now tell me how you know Fuentes."

"We were lovers."

Uh-oh! Had Claire heard that? With all that had happened in the past few moments, Jordan had almost forgotten she was still transmitting. Obviously Esteban hadn't. Darting a quick glance in the general direction of Jordan's left ear, he added a caveat.

"It was long ago. Very long ago, when Maria and I attended Pompeu Fabra University in Barcelona. We saw little of each other in the years since, but remained good friends. I am godfather to her son."

Luis and this Fuentes woman must have been *very* good friends, Jordan thought, for her to name an ex-lover as her son's godfather. Wondering about TJ's connection to the woman, she jumped into the conversation.

"Who is this Fuentes?"

Esteban bit out a reply. "She was an agent for the Organization of American States Counter-Smuggling Initiative."

"Was?"

"The *federales* gunned her down a few years ago. They didn't know she was undercover or that she was working an op with your DEA. Few did, including her family."

There seemed to be a lot of that going around, Jordan thought with a small huff.

"Maria told me about you." Esteban's intent gaze returned to TJ. "She said you were a good man. She said you were to be trusted."

"Funny, she didn't say the same about you. In fact, I don't recall that she ever mentioned your name."

"She would have no reason to. As I said, we saw each little in recent years and I prefer to operate independently since my retirement from the military."

"We have a name for cowboys like you."

Esteban permitted himself a small smile. His lips curving under the thick black mustache, he dipped his head in acknowledgment.

"I've heard them all. If we must resort to labels, I prefer soldier of fortune."

"Is that why you're on the payroll of the emerald cartel? To make your fortune?"

"And to avenge Maria's death."

"You said *federales* killed her," TJ reminded him. "You planning to exact vengeance from the Colombian government?"

"I plan to confirm the identity of the man who lured her into that trap and kill him."

The colonel said it with such complete assurance that Jordan didn't doubt his quarry would be fertilizer in a matter of weeks, if not days.

"It would appear, Scott, that my goal coincides with yours. And," he added with a nod toward Jordan, "that of the so delightful, so lovely Diamond."

TJ's gaze sliced to Jordan. "He knows your code name? The organization you work for?"

She could see he didn't appreciate the fact that Esteban was apparently privy to highly confidential information *he'd* only learned last night.

"As far as I know," she said, "Luis is one of the good guys. We're running a screen on him now, but I can tell you we share a number of mutual acquaintances. Very high-level, very important people. If they vet him, he's good."

She thought of her Washington contacts, remembered how they'd opened their home to the colonel. Lightning knew the man, too. And Claire, who'd worked an op with him in San Antonio. Surely people with their keen instincts couldn't all be wrong in their assessment of the man.

TJ wasn't impressed by her conditional endorsement. His brows snapped together and a steely look came into his eyes. As it turned out, he was questioning more than Esteban's credentials.

"Judging by the way the colonel was sucking on your neck when I arrived on the scene, I'd say you've shared more than a few mutual acquaintances."

The remark pulled Jordan up short. With her mind still churning and her blood pumping from the near shoot-out, she hadn't thought about how that clinch must have appeared to TJ.

"We were just testing the communications."

That sounded as lame to her as it did to TJ. He didn't exactly sneer, but he came close.

"Yeah, sure."

"We were." Jordan didn't particularly like being made to feel like a teenager caught half-naked in the backseat of a car. "And even if we weren't, I don't owe you any explanations."

"You're right. I don't know why I thought last night might have changed things."

Heat crept up Jordan's neck. "Watch it, Scott."

That didn't go down any better than the communications bit. His eyes as flat and cold as iced-over steel, TJ reminded her of their supposed partner status.

"Our respective bosses instructed us to cooperate with each other, remember? So cooperate. Tell me why you let the man Garcia described as his hired gun crawl all over you."

"He did *not* crawl. He just got close enough to talk to Cyrene. My controller," she added in a terse explanation, "who is gathering information and will, hopefully, get back to me at any moment."

"I'm here, Diamond." Claire's cool, crisp voice filled her ear. "Are you ready to copy?"

"Thank God!" Hunching a shoulder, Jordan cupped a hand over her ear. "What have you got?"

"Some rather interesting information. Almost as interesting as what you've just imparted to me."

With both TJ and the colonel glowering at her, Jordan decided to take Cyrene's report in private. She walked a few feet away and turned her back on the two men.

TJ shot silent, angry bullets at her back, fighting

for control. Tension still ratcheted through every inch of his frame. He suspected it wouldn't go away any time soon. The woman was going to kill him!

Last night, she'd knocked him off his rails—literally and figuratively. He'd just about recovered from her disclosures about her secret life when she decided they should blow away old hurts and left-over desire with sex. Just sex.

Sometime between midnight and dawn, TJ had realized that he wanted a whole lot more than sex from this woman. What, he didn't know. He was still trying to figure that out when the fire alarm went off this morning and the security cameras had kicked on to reveal Jordan kneeling beside a choking, gasping boy.

TJ had seen another side of her then. Coolheaded, rock steady, in control. He hadn't had time yet to as-similate this new Jordan, get her fixed in his head.

Now he had to factor in a whole new aspect that centered on an agent with the code name Diamond. TJ had just about busted a gut when the woman had ignored his relayed order and strolled out on the deck with Garcia's cohort. Not two minutes later, her supposedly secure transmission had erupted into static.

He'd waited, his heart measuring every second, then decided to go in. He wouldn't forget the sheer terror that had knifed into him when he'd spotted Jordan bent backward over that rail, fighting off an attacker.

Only he hadn't been an attacker.

And she hadn't been fighting.

His jaw locking, TJ turned to Esteban. He didn't buy that bull about the Cartozan being Maria's old lover or wanting to avenge her death. Maybe because he didn't *want* to buy it. What he wanted was to make raw hamburger meat out of the man's face.

The suspicion and hostility emanating from TJ in waves didn't seem to concern the colonel. Smiling, the older man retrieved a silver cigarette case from the railing behind him and clicked it open.

"If it makes a difference," he said amiably, holding out the case, "I didn't know Jordan was your woman."

"Now you do." Selecting one of the short, thin cigarillos, TJ rolled it between his fingers. "I suggest you keep that in mind next time you decide to, how did Jordan phrase it? Test communications."

Chuckling, Esteban selected a cigarillo for himself and sniffed the outer wrapping appreciatively before lighting both his and TJ's.

"This controller Jordan speaks with. Cyrene. She is *my* woman. Or will be, when I convince her she cannot continue to hold me at bay."

The information put a lid on some of TJ's instinctive hostility. His suspicion remained intact until Jordan rejoined them. Her attention was all on Esteban.

"Cyrene got hold of the chief of the OAS's

Counter-Smuggling Task Force. He says he's had no contact with you about Special Agent Maria Fuentes."

Unperturbed, the Cartozan exhaled a thin stream of smoke. "That's true. He has not."

"But Chameleon has."

"Ahhh, Chameleon." A smile warmed the man's chocolate-brown eyes. "Were it not for Cyrene, I might yet try to tempt the delectable Chameleon to sin."

"Like that's going to happen," Jordan retorted.

TJ had had it with all these code names. "What's the bottom line here?" he asked impatiently. "Is the colonel playing a double game with us or his Colombian bosses?"

"According to *my* bosses, he's working his own agenda, but we can trust him."

If TJ had learned anything during his years undercover, it was never to take a stranger's word for anything. But this word came from Jordan, who he did trust. Mostly.

He couldn't shake the nagging little worry that this hunger for her had clouded his judgment. And the bigger worry that he was fast losing control of this op. There were too many players in the game now. So he wasn't real happy when Jordan announced another.

"Just so you know," she said to Esteban. "Cyrene won't be acting as my controller for this mission any longer."

"May I inquire why?"

"She's going into the field."

TJ swore under his breath. That's all he needed. Another new arrival at the Tranquility Institute he'd have to keep on his radar screen. Esteban didn't appear to like the news any more than TJ did.

"Why does she go into the field?" the colonel asked, frowning.

"She thinks she might be able to get close to one of Bartholomew's clients. The man left the institute suddenly this morning, still hauling unresolved grief issues over the death of his wife and son. Cyrene's flying out to L.A. and will intercept him at the airport when he lands."

Esteban's frown deepened. "She goes to intercept a courier for Bartholomew Greene?"

"We don't know he's a courier. We just want to know why he left the institute so suddenly. He booked the last seat on the turnaround of the flight you and Garcia arrived on."

The colonel let loose with a string of Spanish oaths. His jaw tight, he shot his cigarillo over the railing.

"Tell Claire she must not intercept this man!"

Jordan's brows lifted. "I beg your pardon."

"Tell her she puts herself in danger. Tell her…" With an impatient shake of his head, he reached out and snagged her arm. "No, no. I will tell her myself."

"Hey!"

Ignoring her protest, he pulled her closer. The

move jolted TJ into action. He was damned if he was going to stand there and let this man bury his face in Jordan's neck again.

He'd taken a single step in their direction when he picked up the sound of voices in the conference room. Moving fast, he clamped a hand over Esteban's forearm.

"Back off, Colonel."

"I know she is your woman. I merely wish to protect mine."

"Hey!" Jordan said again. "You need to watch those possessive adjectives."

"Garcia's coming," TJ hissed.

Muttering another curse, Esteban released Jordan and assumed a casual pose at the railing. When Garcia, Myers and Greene strolled out onto the veranda a few seconds later, the colonel was relating a story from his days as head of the Cartozan Special Forces.

"So, I sent a heavily armed Delta squad against the intruders who had breached our supposedly impenetrable defenses. Imagine our chagrin when the squad surrounded two boys on a donkey. *Los muchachos* had managed to find the one centimeter of perimeter where our very expensive, very sensitive sensors did not overlap."

TJ forced a chuckle. "I'll bet those were very two surprised boys."

"Two very relieved boys by the time we delivered them to their parents. Ah, there you are, Alejandro.

Have you and Bartholomew concluded negotiations?"

"We have."

The negotiations must have gone well, Jordan thought, observing the three men closely. Bartholomew looked like a cat that just lapped up a whole bowl of cream. Garcia had a spring to his step. Even the dour Myers wore a smile. She was filing the information away for a later report, when Garcia's inquiring glance settled on TJ.

"I don't believe we've met."

"Thomas Jackson Scott. I'm chief of security here at the Tranquility Institute."

"TJ recently joined our staff." Bartholomew clapped a hand on his employee's shoulder. "In the few weeks he's been with us, he's upgraded our physical security and put all kinds of new procedures in place."

"How fortunate you found someone so skilled."

"Yes, it was." Genial and expansive, Bartholomew played the gracious host for his Colombian guest. "I hope you'll stay at the institute for a few days to rest after your long flight."

Garcia declined with seemingly real regret. "As much as I would love to, I'm afraid Luis and I must depart immediately. I'm delivering another shipment to a dealer in Hong Kong. Duncan's suggestion that we stop in Hawaii en route was most fortuitous."

"For both of us," Bartholomew concurred. "And for you, Jordan. Alejandro called his superiors from my office. They agreed to your price."

Big surprise there, she thought cynically. They probably would have agreed to half of what she'd offered just to keep their good buddy Bartholomew happy.

Garcia took her hand in both of his to seal the deal. "May I say it is a pleasure doing business with such a beautiful woman? You must visit the Muzo mine sometime to see the source of your stones."

"I'd like that. I toured the diamond mines in Brazil and found the trip very instructive. When do you return from Hong Kong? Perhaps I could detour to Colombia on my way back to New York."

Her quick acceptance of the invitation provoked widely different reactions from the five men. Bartholomew beamed in approval. Myers frowned, as though he suspected her of trying to work a better deal on the side. Esteban, standing a little behind the others, telegraphed a quick, silent warning. TJ's expression remained neutral, but Jordan sensed his subtle tension when Garcia extracted a business card and pressed it into her hand.

"We spend only one night in Hong Kong. If you could fly into Bogotá on Friday, I would be most happy to take you up to the mine."

That would give Jordan two more days to snoop around the institute. If she didn't uncover a link between Greene and his suspected involvement in money laundering at this end, maybe she'd have more luck at the other.

"Friday works for me. Assuming Bartholomew

doesn't mind me hanging around here for a few more days."

Her host rushed to reassure her on that point. "After what you did for young Davy this morning, you're more than welcome to remain as my guest for as long as you like. Now I think we should all celebrate the latest addition to my private collection. Surely you have time for a drink before you leave, Alejandro."

"But of course."

"Jordan, Luis, TJ...will you join us?"

Bartholomew led the way back inside, Myers and Garcia with him. Jordan started to follow, only to find her egress blocked by Luis Esteban. His eyes hot and fierce, he leaned in close.

"Stay away from the Muzo mine," he whispered, his voice low and urgent. "It's too dangerous. And tell Claire she is not to run that intercept!"

Chapter 12

"That's all he said? I'm not to run the intercept?"

Swinging between amusement and annoyance, Claire keyed up the volume on the speaker. Diamond's face filled the wall-size screen on the opposite wall, beamed into OMEGA's control center by the miniaturized camera embedded in her laptop.

"That's all he said," Diamond confirmed. "He departed the institute with Garcia right after that, so I didn't get a chance to determine whether the order was directed to you as an operative or—" she paused, her nose wrinkling "—as his woman."

The comment provoked an exasperated huff from Claire. That pretty well summed up her long-standing, if tenuous, relationship with Colonel Luis Esteban. Steeped in traditional values, the Latin American kept trying to separate the woman from the agent. One he wanted to adore and cherish. The other he felt obligated to protect. He had yet to accept that Claire felt supremely comfortable in both skins and required neither adoration nor protection.

"I suspect it was the latter," Claire said. "Luis tends toward the center on the IAS scale."

"And that is?"

"A measurement of psychological inertia, activation and stability."

"I'll take your word for that. Are you sure you have time to make it to L.A.?"

Claire glanced at the bank of clocks above the screen. It was 8:10 p.m. D.C. time, 3:10 p.m. in Hawaii.

McShay had booked a first-class seat on the turn-around of the same flight Garcia and Luis had arrived on. After some fast, behind-the-scenes maneuvering between OMEGA, the FAA and the parent airline, the aircraft had experienced a "mechanical delay" and departed Hawaii just moments ago.

Factoring the time zone changes and flying time into the equation, Claire had almost four hours to get outfitted, jump into the slick little air force jet standing by for her and make the intercept in L.A. She could do it. If she hustled.

"I'll make it, Diamond. Rigger will act as your controller while I'm in the field."

The lanky Oklahoman whose code name stemmed from his early years in the oil fields moved into the camera's angle. "I've got you, Diamond. You're in good hands."

"I'll touch base with you after I make contact with McShay," Claire advised.

"Roger that."

Jordan paused again. The ultra-high-definition camera picked up the faint wrinkle in her brow as she issued a friendly warning.

"Luis wasn't just firing for effect. Be careful out there, Cyrene."

"The same goes for you."

Regret tugged at Claire as she relinquished control to Rigger. Jordan was a friend as well as a fellow agent. She hated to pass her off in the middle of an operation, but a steady sense of purpose outweighed that reluctance. She was eminently well qualified to run this intercept, both personally and professionally.

Claire knew firsthand the devastation of losing a spouse. Her husband's brutal murder had occurred years ago, long before OMEGA recruited her, but the pain was still there, buried just under her breastbone. Looking back, she could remember the emotions that had wracked her.

She'd learned to deal with her shock and anger and bouts of depression. And the loneliness. The horrible, wrenching loneliness. To help her through those awful years, she'd turned her trained psychologist's mind to the process of grieving itself. The insights she'd acquired hadn't erased the pain but did allow her to put her emotions into a framework she could understand and accept.

From the information she'd gathered on Harry McShay, the computer magnate hadn't achieved either understanding or acceptance. Getting close to him would require patience and skill. Claire possessed both.

Thankfully she'd packed a change of clothes before assuming her duties as Diamond's controller. Jeans and a cotton cable-knit sweater were fine for long hours at the control desk, monitoring a field agent's activities and compiling information on request. This particular activity required something more sophisticated.

The ice-blue pantsuit was a fine merino wool, perfect for what had turned into a blustery April evening. The color complemented her pale blond hair. Tossing a Burberry raincoat lined with the new, fashionable pink plaid over her arm, she headed for the elevator that would whisk her down to Technical Ops. Mackenzie had come in to outfit Claire personally for this mission. While his wife did her thing, Nick waited in his office on the ground floor of the town house for a final outbrief.

Mackenzie inserted a thin, flat disk into the shoulder strap of Claire's purse.

"This is the absolute latest in flat-screen digital

imaging. You won't believe the resolution on the pictures this baby picks up. The sound's not bad, either."

Mac was at her computer, programming the disk, when the Tech Ops door whooshed open and a wind-blown Maggie Sinclair rushed in.

"Good! I caught you."

The agent known as Chameleon thrust a hand through her tangled chestnut hair. The years Maggie had spent in the field and at head of OMEGA sat as easily on her as did marriage and motherhood. Her brown eyes sparkled, her skin glowed and the tiny wrinkles at the corners of her eyes only added character to an already arresting face.

"I know you've only got a few minutes," she said with a smile that included both Claire and Mackenzie. "So do I. Nick agreed to stand guard over my tribe while I zipped up to talk to you."

"You brought the girls and the baby?"

"The girls are with Adam for a father-daughter night at the theater. I brought the baby and the animals. We're on our way back from the vet. Don't ask," she warned with a rueful grimace.

"Oh, Lord!"

That came from Mackenzie, who regularly baby-sat for Maggie's rapidly expanding brood. Claire merely shuddered. She could only imagine the chaos downstairs as Nick tried to control the lively two-year-old Maggie had birthed right there in her old office, the monstrous Hungarian sheepdog she'd inherited from the vice president and the diabolical, purple-and-orange-striped iguana she'd acquired during a mission in Central America.

The iguana had been a gift from Luis Esteban, the man who was now apparently very much on Chameleon's mind.

"I've been thinking about Luis since you called a while ago," she said, hitching a hip on the corner of Mackenzie's desk. "I worked with him in Cartoza. You worked with him in San Antonio. You've also kept him on a pretty long leash since then."

"He's not ready for a short one," Claire said calmly.

"That's what I wanted to talk to you about. Luis and his amours. This woman, this Maria Fuentes. You checked her out?"

"I did. As Luis said, they studied at a university in Barcelona together. Indications are they also engaged in a torrid affair that lasted for several years afterward."

"So torrid he would risk his life to avenge hers?"

Claire had been asking herself the same thing for the past few hours. Had Luis told Jordan the truth? Or had he gone over to the enemy?

Her years as a psychologist, trained to ask rather than answer, prompted her to turn the question around. "What do you think? You've known him longer than I have, Maggie. He makes no secret of the fact that he carried a torch for you for years."

"Until he met you."

"The flame still flickers every once in a while," Claire returned with a smile. Luis's past loves didn't threaten her. They'd shaped him into the man he now was, just as her love for her husband had shaped her.

"Yes, well, I think that may be the crux of the matter."

Maggie swung her leg encased in denim. The jeans were spotted with something that looked suspiciously like iguana spit to Claire. She'd had one or two encounters with the repulsive creature herself.

"Luis is hardly the gentle, sensitive type. If he loved this woman—if he loved *any* woman—he'd consider it his sworn duty to avenge a wrong done to her no matter how long it took or what danger it involved."

Mackenzie emitted a snort. "Ha! You've just described every male in OMEGA."

"True," Maggie conceded, laughing. "So true! We wouldn't have them any other way, the big lugs."

"Speaking of big lugs…" Mackenzie handed Claire back her shoulder bag. "What's the story on this DEA agent Jordan's working with? Nick says they have a history."

Claire's natural reticence and respect for a fellow agent's privacy battled with her close kinship with these women. She settled for a shrug and half answer.

"I suspect Jordan and Scott may also have something of a present. Look, I've got to get down and talk to Nick, then head out to the airport. He can fill you in on how Jordan's handling this TJ Scott."

If someone had asked her several hours later, Jordan would have said TJ wasn't handling well at all.

He'd bent her ear for a good hour after Garcia and Esteban departed. He was still torqued over the scene on the veranda, but more concerned about the risks associated with her proposed trip to Colombia. Now he'd appeared uninvited at her cottage to reiterate his objections.

"We have a man at Muzo, working undercover with Colombian moles." He paced the sitting room, edgy and impatient. "You don't need to go in."

Jordan hooked a heel on the chintz cushion and wrapped her arms around her upraised knee. Her sleeveless peach blouse and linen slacks were hopelessly wrinkled after the long day, but TJ hadn't given her time to change before showing up at her bungalow. Drawing on her rapidly diminishing store of patience, she shrugged.

"I won't step on any DEA toes while I'm in Colombia."

"Dammit, Jordan, this isn't about protecting turf. This is about a valley that's so inaccessible you have to drive up to twelve thousand feet and plunge straight down again on a narrow road carved out of sheer rock, dodging guerrillas and bandits the whole way. They've ambushed convoys consisting of more than fifty armed vehicles."

"You've made the trip?"

"No, I haven't." Frustrated, he raked a hand through his hair. "But I've talked to others who have and they say it's not an excursion for the faint of heart."

"In case you haven't noticed, Scott, I'm not faint of anything."

That fired him up again. His neck reddening above the collar of his shirt, he didn't hold back.

"I've noticed, all right. I've also noticed you're stubborn as hell and as much of a cowboy as your friend, the colonel. You pull another stunt like the one this afternoon, when you deliberately put yourself in harm's way and we'll renegotiate this so-called partnership real fast."

Jordan swallowed a sigh. She was going into Muzo. End of story. She certainly didn't intend to spend the next two days arguing about it. Nor did she intend to waste those two days twiddling her thumbs.

A quick check of her watch told her Claire should make contact with McShay at any moment. Hopefully, the widower would prove the link between Greene and the large-scale money transactions he was suspected of facilitating. In the meantime, Jordan was feeling as antsy and restless as TJ.

Her foot hit the floor. Uncurling, she pushed off the sofa. "I know you're spoiling for a fight. Sorry.

I'm not giving you one. Not tonight. But I do have a suggestion on how we could burn up some of our energy."

His chin jerked up. The air around him took on an electric charge. When he closed the short distance between them and tunneled a hand under her hair, Jordan realized he'd seriously misinterpreted her comment.

"Whoa! I'm not talking about another romp."

"Maybe you're not. I am."

Obviously. She could see the heat flaring in his eyes, feel the tension in the body so close to hers. An answering need slammed into Jordan, so swift and all consuming she lost her bearings for a few moments. All she could think of, all she could imagine, were TJ's mouth and hands roaming her bare flesh.

"We said we weren't going to do this, remember?" To her disgust, her words spilled out fast and breathless. "Even though last night was just sex, we said—"

"It wasn't just sex."

"What was it, then?"

"Damned if I know." His hand tightened on her nape. "I can tell you this much, Red. I tried to get you out of my head three years ago and never quite succeeded. You were always there, at the back of my mind. Along with regret and a whole heap of guilt for dragging you into that mess. After last night, the guilt's pretty much gone, and I've decided I can live with the regret."

"So what's the problem?"

"I can't figure out which was worse. Wanting you then, knowing I couldn't have you, or wanting you now and not knowing how to make it right this time."

She'd been burned once. Caution dictated that she take it slow and careful this round.

"Why don't we try a phased approach? See what feels right, what doesn't?"

"Starting when?"

"Starting now. This is phase one."

Lifting her hands, she framed TJ's face. His cheeks bristled with an after-five shadow. Beneath the whiskers, his skin warmed her palms.

"Just follow my lead."

Rising onto the balls of her feet, she brought her mouth to his. The feel of him, the taste and scent and smooth, slick warmth of him, quivered through her.

She took her time. She wanted this to be slow and tantalizing and delicious, unlike the frenzy that had gripped them last night—and every other time they'd come together, now that she thought about it.

She got what she wanted. TJ rested his hands lightly on her hips and let her explore his mouth with hers. Her teeth scraped his lower lip, nipping gently. Her tongue teased the velvety warmth beyond.

Remembering what one kiss had led to last night, Jordan conducted a fierce, silent debate. She wanted more. Just a little more.

Drawing back, she tested the waters. "Don't take

this the wrong way, okay? I'm not suggesting we
jump a couple of steps. But how would you feel
about a little body contact during this phase?"

He creased his forehead and gave the matter
solemn consideration. "I think I can handle it. Just
go easy on me."

Smiling, she leaned into a loose embrace. The
tension kicked up a notch. So did her hunger. But
the overall sensation was one of deliciously height-
ened awareness.

Like in one of Bartholomew's meditation sessions, she thought wryly. She could almost hear him
instructing her to close her eyes, free her thoughts,
concentrate on her physical state.

Her lids drifted shut. Her world narrowed. Her
pulse picked up speed.

Now Bartholomew would tell her to think about
the world around her. Feel the breeze on her heated
skin. Hear the surf pounding with the same relent-
less rhythm as her heart. He'd urge her to let the
sounds and colors and shapes come to her. Broaden
her. Stimulate her.

Suddenly, her eyes flew open. The urgent prodding against her belly told her she wasn't the only
one who'd been stimulated. Feeling a distinct kinship with the horny Felicity Waller-Winston, Jordan
pulled away.

"I think that's enough for phase one."

Hardly!

TJ managed to swallow the swift retort. He even

managed to hook his thumbs in his pockets instead
of hauling Jordan into the bedroom and streaking
straight to phase four or five. The effort damn near
doubled him over. His only consolation was that
she looked as hot and bothered as he felt at the
moment.

"That was good," he said, eyeing her flushed face
and disordered hair. "Very good. But it generated
more energy than it burned."

"Actually, I had something else in mind when I
suggested burning up energy."

"Like what?"

"I want into Bartholomew's treasure room."

That took the P out of his Peter. Snapping back
to reality, TJ shook his head. "Not possible."

"You know the security system. You must know
how to bypass it."

"That vault is better protected than a Minuteman
III silo."

"Are you saying you can't get in?"

"I'm saying you don't need to get in. I've scoped
it out, Red."

"Ha! I thought so."

"Aside from an emerald phallus, I didn't find
anything interesting. Certainly no evidence that
linked Greene to a pesos-for-dollars operation."

"When was this?"

"Shortly after I signed on as director of security."

"The Star of the East was stolen just two weeks
ago," she reminded him.

"I know. I was planning to go back in for another look when I could work it."

"Work it tonight."

"It's too risky, Jordan. I covered myself last time by scheduling a routine system check. I used the downtime to cross a few wires and slip inside the vault for a quick look around."

"Bartholomew just acquired an expensive new toy," she said, using that as a springboard. "You can advise your security monitor that you want to run an unscheduled system check to make sure his new bauble is secure. My marching orders come from the president," she added when he shook his head. "Would you rather call him and explain why you don't want to cross a few wires for me?"

The polite query hung on the air for a good five seconds. Finally TJ unlocked his jaw.

"I'm beginning to think Esteban had the right idea."

"About?"

"About keeping his woman naked and chained to a bed for the rest of her natural life."

"Dear, God!" Jordan steepled her palms and rolled her eyes toward heaven. "*Puh-leez* let me be in the general vicinity if Luis ever says something like that to Claire."

Chapter 13

The timing worked out perfectly. The sleek little air force jet put Claire into LAX a good fifteen minutes before the jumbo jet from Hawaii lumbered in.

She was at the gate when the passengers deplaned and ID'd McShay immediately. He was thinner than he'd appeared in the magazine and newspaper articles she'd pulled up on him, but she could hardly mistake the bulldog face featured on the front cover of *Time* magazine.

She also ID'd the federal agent tailing him. Coordination between OMEGA and DEA had improved dramatically in the past few days, so she knew to look for a tanned tourist in shorts, sandals and flashy tropical shirt.

The agent had reported no contact between Garcia and McShay at the airport in Hawaii. The Colombian had arrived, picked up a rental car and driven straight to the institute. McShay had waited in the first-class lounge for his flight to be called. He'd grown restless during the two-hour "mechanical" delay and made several calls on his cell phone. Now he faced another delay because of a missed connection to Oakland and his home in the Bay Area.

With an almost imperceptible nod to the agent, Claire joined the throng of passengers streaming away from the gate. As anticipated, McShay headed directly for the first-class lounge. She followed him in.

"My flight from Hawaii just arrived," he informed one of the hostesses manning the marble reception counter. "I missed my connection and need to be rebooked."

She checked his ticket and began clicking her keyboard. "We'll get you fixed up right away, Mr. McShay."

Claire passed her ticket to the second receptionist and shared a smile with the man next to her.

"Aren't these delays annoying?"

"Very."

"You're all set, Dr. Cantwell." The second hostess slid Claire's ticket across the marble counter and checked the bank of clocks on the wall. "We should call the flight to Oakland in about forty minutes."

"Thank you."

The attendant assisting McShay clicked her keyboard again. "I've booked you on that same flight, sir. Here's your new boarding pass."

"Thanks." He slid the ticket into the pocket of his lightweight sport coat. "One of my associates flew out of LAX earlier today. He was supposed to leave a message here for me."

"Let me check."

Claire's heart bumped. She moved away from the counter but kept the target in sight. When the receptionist passed him a folded sheet of notepaper, her heart thumped again.

Reining in her excitement, she waited while McShay slipped the note into his suit pocket and settled into one of the leather armchairs by the windows. She claimed a seat a short distance away, then sorted through the newspapers displayed on the coffee table. Pretending not to find the one she wanted, she glanced at the paper on the table beside McShay's chair.

"Is that the *New York Times?*"

He checked the banner and nodded. "Yes."

"Are you going to read it?"

"No, you're welcome to it."

He got up to deliver the paper at the same time a steward appeared to take Claire's drink order.

"I'll have a black Russian," she told him. "Light on the Kahlúa, please."

"And you, sir?"

McShay didn't respond. His expression had gone flat, his lips thin and tight. The overhead fluorescent lighting gave his fleshy face a grayish cast and emphasized the dark circles under his eyes.

"Sir?"

The computer mogul gave a little jerk, as if coming out of a trance. "Scotch," he said gruffly. "Straight up. Make it a double. Here's your *Times.*"

Claire took the newspaper and voiced a gentle concern. "Are you all right?"

"Yes. I just… That is…" He blew out a breath and swiped a palm over his face. "My wife rarely drank. When she did, she always ordered a black Russian."

Claire had unearthed that bit of information just hours ago. She disliked using the details she'd dug up about his wife like this. Playing on McShay's grief went against her training and her natural instinct to comfort and heal. Unfortunately, death formed a common bond between them.

"I lost my husband eight years ago," she said quietly. "I still bleed a little this time of year, whenever I catch the baseball scores on radio or TV. Bill and I met at a Yankees game."

"Eight years. Does it take that long for the hurt to go away?"

"It never goes away. You just learn to accept it and understand that the loss of someone you love shapes you into a very different person from the one you were before."

"That's what Bartholomew says."

"Bartholomew?"

"My therapist. Dr. Bartholomew Greene."

"Of the Greene Tranquility Institute?"

"Do you know him?"

"I know of him," Claire said with perfect truth. "I'm a psychologist. I've studied his methodology. Did you find his combination of transpersonal meditation and stone therapy helpful in dealing with your grief?"

With a harsh laugh, McShay unbuttoned his suit coat and pulled back a flap to reveal a square-cut emerald tiepin. "I never go anywhere without this stone. Bartholomew made a believer out of me. He and his teachings are what got me through the past few years."

"Really? I'd love to hear a firsthand description of his practices. Would you care to join me?"

He hesitated for several moments. Claire suspected the envelope she could see poking out of the inside pocket of his jacket pulled him in one direction, his urge to sing Bartholomew's praises in another.

"My name's Claire, by the way." Smiling, she offered her hand. "Claire Cantwell."

"Harry McShay."

The human touch overcame his hesitation. Dropping into the chair next to hers, he launched into a paean to the guru of Greene.

Claire kept him talking until the hostess called their flight. They boarded the small commuter jet together. Since first class consisted of only two rows, she and McShay were seated side by side.

She handed her folded raincoat and overnight bag to the flight attendant for stowing. Itching to get her hands on that note, Claire hoped McShay would do the same with his suit coat. Unfortunately, he declined the attendant's offer and kept the lightweight jacket on for the duration of the short flight, most of which was spent discussing Bartholomew Greene's methods and teachings.

When they touched down at Oakland, Claire made a casual offer. "I'm staying at the Radisson. If you're heading in that direction, I'll be happy to share a taxi."

"Thanks, but I have a car waiting."

Nodding, she draped her folded raincoat over her arm and slung her purse over her shoulder. She knew when to push and when to let common courtesy do her work for her. McShay made the counteroffer a moment later.

"The Radisson is right on my way," he said with only the barest hint of reluctance. "I could drop you there."

"Are you sure? I don't want to inconvenience you."

"You won't."

"Okay, thanks."

Tucking a wayward silver-blond strand into the smooth coil at the base of her neck, Claire waited for the aircraft door to open.

They were the first passengers to deplane. McShay matched his stride to hers as they headed for the baggage-claim area. Two gates down she spotted the agent she'd been advised would pick up the tail in Oakland. He fell in behind them, looking very much like a college professor in his tweed jacket and neatly trimmed white beard.

Once on the escalator, McShay reached into his jacket pocket for the note. Claire caught the movement from the corner of her eye. Angling around, she watched him extract a folded sheet of paper.

Claire was one step down. She couldn't see what was written on it, but it had to be a phone number. Referring to the paper, McShay unclipped his cell phone and flipped up the lid.

Thank goodness for Mackenzie's high-tech wizardry. With seeming nonchalance, Claire aimed her purse strap at the cell phone. She knew the bug would pick up the faint beeps as McShay punched in the numbers and beam them back to OMEGA. Rigger would trace the number within minutes.

"This is McShay. I'm down. Bring the car around."

Claire willed her expression to remain calm as her target steered her through the baggage-claim area toward the exit.

Once outside, they were met by a chilly April night. Fingers of cold, misty fog drifted in from the bay, forming a hazy halo effect around the flood-lights in the passenger-pickup area.

Claire felt a shudder ripple through her. It was more nerves than cold, but she didn't argue when McShay suggested she put on her raincoat.

"Here, let me help you."

"Thanks."

He shook out the folds and held it up for her. Claire fished around behind her for a moment but couldn't find the armholes. When she glanced over her shoulder, the glare of oncoming headlights showed that McShay's face had gone dead white.

"Harry?" She whirled around. "What's the matter?"

"My daughter went nuts over pink." The words came out raw and jagged, as though his throat was stuffed with shards of glass. His hand trembling, he smoothed a palm over the pink plaid lining of her Burberry coat. "I brought her gloves and a hat made out of this same plaid on our last trip to London."

Guilt stabbed into Claire. She hadn't picked up that piece of information when she'd run screens on the man's wife and daughter. If she had, would she have used it as another weapon in her arsenal? God, she hoped not.

She laid a hand on his arm, driven by a need to comfort but distracted by the swish of a car pulling up to the curb.

"It's all right, Harry."

The vehicle door opened. A figure dressed in black emerged from the idling car. With one eye on the driver rounding the front fender, Claire squeezed McShay's arm and repeated the age-old palliative.

"It's all right."

"No, it's not!" Exploding into fury, he threw back his arm. "It'll never be all right again!"

His sudden fury was symptomatic of phase two in the grief process. At any other time, Claire would have responded with unimpaired calm to the "why me?" frustration and rage.

Unfortunately, she didn't have time to respond at all. McShay's violent movement had jerked her off balance. She pitched forward, ramming into his chest. A second later, all hell broke loose.

Seeing what he must have thought was a struggle, the driver spit out a curse and dropped into a crouch. Claire heard a shout, another curse, the thud of pounding feet. She shoved away from McShay and swung around an instant before the percussive shock of a .45 Magnum fired at close range assaulted her eardrums.

"Get down, Harry!"

She threw herself to the pavement, dragging her Springfield SD subcompact from her purse on the way down. Before she could thumb the safety, the driver had pumped out two more rounds. Answering shots came from behind Claire, pinging into the car's fender, shattering its windshield.

The gunfire stampeded the crowd waiting in the pickup area. They couldn't see who was doing the shooting, weren't sure where the shots had come from. Screaming and shouting, they ran for whatever cover they could find.

In the midst of the chaos, the driver jumped back into the car. It screeched away from the curb, accelerating wildly. Claire scrambled up and aimed at the rear tire, then bit out a curse as the tweedy college professor got between her and the fleeing vehicle. Assuming a two-fisted shooter's stance, the agent fired three quick shots. The first crystallized the rear window. The second plowed into the trunk. The third ignited the gas tank.

The car burst into a fireball. The explosion lifted the vehicle a good four feet off the concrete before slamming it back down again. Metal twisted. Hydraulic lines hissed. Flames leaped through shattered windows.

Seared by the heat, Claire whirled around to check on McShay. Her heart dropped to her feet when she saw him lying in a pool of blood and gore. The top half of his skull was blown away.

Jordan got the news as she waited for TJ to arrive at her bungalow with the schematics of the vault. He had insisted she wait until 4:00 a.m. to attempt the penetration. Everyone should be asleep at that hour, including Bartholomew, who had a habit of making late-night visits to the vault to fondle, drool over or otherwise play with his treasures.

The plan was for TJ to relieve the officer monitoring the security screens and send him to conduct a perimeter check. Monkeying with the system so a shutdown wouldn't trigger an alarm would take TJ a good ten minutes. That left Jordan an estimated twenty to get in, snoop around the vault and get out again.

She was pacing the sitting room, impatient to get her hands on those schematics, when her earring began to vibrate. Excitement shot through her. This was probably Rigger, contacting her with the results of Claire's intercept.

"Diamond here. What have you got for me?"

"'Fraid you're not gonna like it," Rigger responded. "The intercept went sour. Cyrene's okay, but she's got two DBs on her hands."

Oh, hell! Two dead bodies. From the sound of it, the intercept went *way* sour!

"Was one of those DBs McShay?" Jordan asked.

"Roger that."

"What happened?"

"Cyrene made contact with McShay at LAX. There was a message waiting for him in the first-class lounge. He opened it after they landed at Oakland and called to request a car be brought around."

"Did Cyrene copy the number he called?"

"She did. It checks to a scumbag by the name of Rodrigo Herrera, who we assume is the crispy critter lying beside McShay in the morgue right now. Apparently Herrera got spooked during the handoff of the vehicle and started blasting with his .45. He put one of the rounds into McShay's head."

"On purpose?"

"We don't know. The agent tailing Cyrene and the target took Herrera out. He also took out the vehicle and everything in it. The techies are shifting through the ashes now, but initial indications are the trunk contained upwards of a quarter million in U.S. dollars."

So Jordan's gut feeling about McShay had proved right. The man *had* left the Tranquility Institute with more than meditation on his mind. The knowledge didn't give her any particular satisfaction. Especially since they still hadn't made the link directly back to Greene.

"You're sure Cyrene's okay?"

"She's pissed at the way things went down, but okay. She said to tell you she's going to stay in California and work the connection between McShay and Herrera."

"Anything else?"

"Nope, that's it."

"Keep me posted on those sifting ashes."

"Will do."

TJ arrived at her bungalow a short while later. "Did you get word about McShay?" he asked, thumping the rolled schematics against his thigh.

"Yes."

"What's the take on your end?"

"We're not sure yet. Could be Herrera was going to hand McShay the keys and let him deposit that trunkful of cash. Could be he was delivering signature cards for new accounts, so he could deposit the quarter of a million himself in McShay's name."

"In either case, they'd need to make deposits in at least twenty-five different accounts to stay under the ten-thousand-dollar ceiling."

"If McShay has upwards of twenty-five bank accounts scattered around the Bay Area," Jordan said with utter conviction, "Cyrene will find them. She's staying in California to work that end of things."

The schematics thumped against TJ's thigh again. "We ran McShay when he first arrived here. He didn't pop in any of our systems."

"Maybe he'll pop in ours. Are those the vault plans?" she asked, itching to get on with her end of things.

"They're for the whole institute."

He spread the drawings on the coffee table and flipped through the sheets until he found the floor plans for the residence. Rolling back the other pages, he anchored them with his hand.

"The vault was constructed the same time as the residence, but Greene has made various improvements and additions over the years."

Hooking her elbows on her knees, Jordan studied the room within a room. It was double-walled in concrete and steel, with its own emergency-power source, air-regeneration capability and fire-suppression systems. Greene and his treasures could probably ride out a category five hurricane in comfort and safety. The electrical-wiring diagram looked like spaghetti.

TJ leaned forward, his shoulder prodding Jordan's. She felt the warmth of his flesh, followed by swift annoyance that the mere brush of his skin against hers could distract her so easily. Frowning, she hunched her shoulders and forced herself to pay attention when TJ thumped a finger against a recent addition.

"Greene added this section to make the display area for the Cross of the Andes. That was done two, three years ago. The new area contains a special beefed-up security shield. I can short-circuit the sound-and-motion sensors, but the heat sensors are integrated into a redundant fire-suppression system. I can't shut them down without taking down the entire halon system, which is monitored by an outside agency."

"I'll be wearing my thermal suit."

And swimming in sweat the whole time.

"Even so, try to avoid the special heat sensors located here, here, and here."

Eyes narrowed in concentration, Jordan memorized the locations. TJ went over the specifics of the vault again before putting that schematic aside to make room for one that included the floor plan for the entire first floor. Jordan zeroed in on Greene's study with its sliding bookshelves and hidden corridor leading to the vault.

The minutes ticked by. She imprinted the drawings onto her brain, room by room, schematic by schematic. A good half hour later, she'd absorbed every detail.

"I'm as ready as I'll ever be."

"I hope so!"

TJ released the rolled-up sheets. When they flopped back down, Jordan fanned through the stack to see what she might have missed. The Meditation Center was there. The spa. The Jade Buddha. Corporate headquarters, with its large, airy conference room.

A small bump-out behind the conference room caught her eye. "What's this?"

"A storage closet. I've checked it out."

"Looks like it backs up against the north wall of the conference room."

"It does."

Jordan pulled up a mental image of that wall. It contained the world map detailing Bartholomew's far-flung empire, with each satellite Tranquility Center designated by an emerald. At its center was the round, unwinking eye marking the headquarters here in Hawaii.

Her heart began to thump. She pulled up another mental image, this one of the Star of the East. Nine hundred-plus carats of emerald in the shape of an oval. Rounded at the top, like the stone dangling between her breasts.

She closed her hand around the teardrop, felt a small shock of vibration. Excitement, she told herself. And sudden, sweeping certainty.

"Change of plans, TJ. I don't think I'll need into the vault after all."

"What?"

"Just get me into that closet."

Chapter 14

With TJ at his security-operations center, covering for the man he'd sent to run a perimeter check, Jordan didn't worry about tripping sensors during her second nocturnal visit to the conference center.

She found the storage closet easily enough. Shining her high-intensity penlight on the rear wall, she moved aside a stack of boxes and thumped the drywall with her knuckles. The first half-dozen thumps sounded solid. The seventh had a hollow ring.

Bingo!

With the penlight clenched between her teeth, Jordan skimmed her fingertips over that section of the wall. Just below the molding she found a soft spot that gave when she pressed it.

A square foot or so of drywall slid noiselessly to one side and there it was. The fabled Star of the East. The stone threw the high-intensity beam from Jordan's penlight back at her in dazzling green rays.

The bulk of the stone lay nested in a special compartment cut into the rear of the conference-room wall. Only a small fraction of its rounded top protruded through to the map. Instead of secreting the famous emerald in the vault with his other treasures, Bartholomew had pulled an Edgar Allan Poe and hidden his purloined stone in plain sight, where he could view and enjoy it every day.

Jordan left it right where it was. She'd located its hiding place. She could retrieve it when necessary. Before she exposed Greene as a thief, she needed to ferret out his link to the lethal drug trade. Sliding the panel back into place, she almost danced into the conference room and aimed her penlight at the center of the map.

"TJ!" she hissed to the nearest security camera. "That's it. The butt end of the Star."

Still flying high, she made her way back to her bungalow. It was black as pitch, with dark clouds obscuring the sky and mountains. She kept an eye out for the security officer TJ had sent to run a perimeter check and her ears tuned to every rustle of the palms. Consequently, she almost jumped out of her synthetic skin when a shadowy figure loomed out of the darkness close to her bungalow.

"It's me," TJ growled.

Swallowing to push her heart back down to her chest, Jordan led the way to the bedroom window they'd left open.

"How the heck did you get here so fast?" she asked, swinging a leg over the windowsill.

"I reset the systems as soon as you were out and recalled my man."

She waited for TJ to follow her inside and close the shutters before switching on a lamp.

"Who would have believed Greene would position the damn thing where everyone could see it?" she exclaimed, dragging back her hood.

"Not me. Obviously."

The reply held more than a trace of self-disgust. Jordan waved an airy hand. She could be magnanimous in victory.

"You would have figured it out sooner or later."

"Yeah, right. Thanks for the vote of confidence. Let's hope I do better with the other half of our mission."

"Okay, here's my thinking on that. If McShay was doing favors for Bartholomew by picking up and/or depositing cash to various bank accounts, there's a chance some of the other guests are, too."

She dragged down the zipper of her thermal suit. She had to get out of it. The damn thing was cooking her.

"We need to have our people scrub the list of

previous guests again," she said, pulling an arm free. "In the meantime, we'll work the ones here."

TJ responded with a grunt.

Jordan glanced up, saw he'd zeroed in on the scraps of lace plastered to her chest. The sweat-soaked fabric clung to her breasts, making a perfect showcase for the puckered nipples at the center.

"Sorry, but my bones are melting. I *have* to shed this thing. I also need to report the find to OMEGA and take a quick shower. Why don't you draw up a list of the guests. We can decide which ones to tackle and how after I clean up."

Pulsing with energy, she headed for the bathroom. On the way, she thumbed her earring. "This is Diamond. Do you read me, Control?"

Rigger came on a few seconds later. "Loud and clear, Diamond. What have you got for me?"

"How about the Star of the East?"

"Come again?"

"She's here. I wrapped my hot little hands around her not ten minutes ago."

"Lightning's gonna be glad to hear that. The prez has been crawling up his back."

Swiftly, Jordan detailed the stone's location and her rationale for leaving it in place. Rigger promised to relay the information to Lightning.

Still buoyed at having accomplished at least part of her mission, she stripped off her soggy underwear and hit the shower. The scent of mango tickled her nostrils as she soaped down. In an admittedly poor imitation of the fabulous Shirley Bassey, Jordan crooned a few bars from the theme of her favorite James Bond movie, "Diamonds are Forever."

The sultry strains drifted from the bathroom to the sitting room. TJ was standing pretty much where Jordan had left him, trying without a whole lot of success to recover from watching her peel off that thermal suit. Although the shower muffled most of the words, he recognized the tune she was humming. Disjointed phrases came to him, sung slightly off key. Diamonds stimulated. Diamonds teased and tantalized. They wouldn't lie or leave a girl in the night. Like men.

A few days ago that line would have pricked TJ's guilt about the way things ended between Jordan and him three years ago. The guilt was gone now, but the hunger had returned in full force. Remembering how she'd looked when he'd surprised her in that shower a few nights ago didn't exactly help matters, either.

TJ could see her. Long and lean and curved in all the right places, her skin as smooth and lustrous as a freshwater pearl.

Sweat popped out on his palms. He shoved his hands in his pockets and told himself to cool it. A few hours ago they'd stood almost where he was standing now and made the conscious decision to take things one step at a time.

He remained where he was for another few moments, arguing, debating, ignoring the ache in his groin. When Jordan got to the line about touching it, stroking it, embracing it, his control snapped.

He strode through the bedroom, shedding shirt and shoes as he went. His pants came off as well. He was naked when he hit the bathroom and fully aroused when Jordan's head whipped around.

She looked him up and down. Mostly down, TJ noted with fierce male satisfaction.

"I thought we decided on a phased approach."

"We did," he agreed, muscling his way into the shower.

"Aren't you skipping a few steps?"

"Nope. This is phase two." Grinning, he plucked the washcloth out of her hand. "Turn around."

When she hesitated, he leaned down and whispered one of the more inventive tricks a couple could perform with a bar of soap, a washcloth and a dirty mind.

"You're making that up!"

"Guess again, Red. Turn around."

Their energetic and decidedly erotic shower activities spilled over into the bedroom.

Maybe it was the thrill of locating the Star of the East. Or the ticking clock that measured the hours remaining before Jordan's imminent departure for Colombia. Whatever the reason, they both ignored the niggling little voice that said it wasn't smart to mix business with pleasure. Especially in their line of work.

By the time they finished, they'd left big water

splotches on the sheets and mattress. Jordan scooted away from the damp spots and snuggled up against TJ's side, intending just a catnap.

She woke an indeterminate time later. She was still curled against his side but had crowded him right to the edge of the bed. He had one foot hooked over hers. The other was planted on the floor to keep from falling off the bed.

Blinking the sleep from her eyes, Jordan studied his profile in the first hazy light of dawn. Amazing how they'd come full circle. The last time she'd shared a bed with this man, his fellow officers had busted down his door. Jordan had been more than half in love with him at the time. An avalanche of anger and disgust had buried that love. Now...

Now what? Did she love him? Did she want him in her life after Hawaii? Did he want her? What the heck was their next step?

She still didn't have the answer to those questions, when he twitched. A moment later his lids lifted. When he turned his head and saw she was awake, a lazy smile came into his gray eyes.

"'Morning, Red. What time is it?"

She raised up enough to squint at the digital clock beside the bed. "Almost six."

"Guess we should get up and get to work."

"Guess so," she agreed, dropping back down beside him.

Neither of them made a move to leave the bed.

The muscles under Jordan's cheek bunched as he bent his arm and played with her tangled hair.

"This morning-after sure beats the last one," he said.

"I was just thinking the same thing."

"Maybe we could try for two out of three."

"Or three out of four. I've got tonight and to-morrow night before I leave for Bogotá."

"I still don't like the idea of you going into the jungles of Colombia without backup."

She pushed up on an elbow, determined to head off another argument. TJ surprised her with a simple declaration.

"I'm going in with you."

"Huh?"

"Bartholomew knows we're old friends. He'll understand when I tell him I don't think it's safe for—"

"For weak, helpless little me to traipse into the jungle without big, strong you to protect me."

His mouth curved. "Something like that."

Jordan pursed her lips, torn between annoyance and a swamping sense of relief. She'd feel a whole lot better going into Muzo with someone she trusted riding shotgun.

And she could understand why TJ would want in on the op. He'd played his role at the Tranquility In-stitute for weeks now with no direct leads or links between Greene and drug money to show for it. Like Jordan, he itched for action.

"In the meantime," he said with a playful slap on her bare rump, "we've got work to do. Move it, woman."

They divided up the guest list over coffee and fresh rolls delivered to the bungalow. TJ disappeared into the bedroom while the waiter delivered the tray, then hogged the single knife to slather butter and strawberry jam over a flaky croissant.

"I'll take Edna and Davy's mom," Jordan said, eyeing the list.

"And Felicity Waller-Winston."

"Sure you don't want to question her?" she asked, straight-faced. "You could probably get more out of her than I could."

"You've had a couple of group sessions with her," TJ countered. "You can get inside her head faster than I can. Besides," he added with a quick, slashing grin, "there's only so much a man should be asked to do for his country."

While they divvied up the rest of the guests, he wolfed down his croissant, a bran muffin, a banana and two cups of coffee. Declining Jordan's amused offer of the other half of her bagel, he rasped a hand across his bristly chin.

"I have to head back to my place, get cleaned up and make morning roll call for my security troops."

Before he slipped out into the still-sleepy dawn, he flicked the teardrop suspended from its thin gold chain.

"Make sure you keep this on. I want to be able to track you."

"Track me how?" she asked, dropping her chin to frown at the emerald.

"We paint all of the stones in Bartholomew's private collection with a chemical compound. All the ones we know about," he corrected with a grimace, obviously thinking of the Star. "The paint is visible only when viewed through special filters."

"And you waited until now to tell me this?"

"Yeah, I did."

"What's the matter, Scott? Didn't you trust me?"

"Just keep this little bauble on, okay? And let me know right away if you pick up anything from the other guests."

"That works both ways," she said tartly.

Nodding, he dropped a quick, hard kiss on her mouth. His unshaven chin scraped hers. Jordan carried the tingle with her when she went to dress.

She'd corner Davy's mom first, she decided, pulling on her gauzy white shorts and a scoop-neck T-shirt sporting the institute's logo. She could tackle Edna and Felicity after group. The rest of the guests on her list she'd hunt down this afternoon.

Although she'd already consumed the half bagel that normally constituted breakfast, Jordan figured she'd find Davy and his mother at the Jade Buddha. She would have to separate Patricia from her son so the two women could talk undisturbed.

She'd suggest a walk along the bluffs, Jordan decided. Use the draw of wanting to know more about asthma and what triggered an attack. After the harrowing experience with Davy yesterday morning, that was no pretext.

As anticipated, Jordan spotted Davy and his mom at a table near the edge of the pool. She started toward them but got only a short way before bony fingers clamped onto her arm.

"Did you hear?" Edna demanded, her voice thick and hoarse. Smeared mascara ringed her reddened eyes, making her look like a fuzzy-haired raccoon.

"Did I hear what?"

"About Harry. Harry McShay. He was shot."

Jordan made a sound somewhere between shock and surprise. She couldn't feign grief for a man she'd only spoken to once or twice in passing.

Edna had spent many more hours with McShay. She appeared to truly mourn her poker partner. Gulping back tears, the widow spilled out the details.

"Felicity went to the reception center a while ago to check the stock report on CNN. She said Harry was gunned down outside the Oakland airport."

She swallowed convulsively. The loose skin of her throat wobbled with each gulp.

"Right at the airport," she whispered, looking horrified.

No, Jordan corrected with a sudden jolt. Not horrified. Terrified. The woman was scared stiff.

"How awful! Was it a robbery?"

"No. Yes. I don't know! I have to talk to Bartholomew about it. I have to tell him—"

On the verge of tears, the widow broke off.

"Tell him what?" Jordan prompted.

"My daughters. I can't… I won't… Oh, God, if anything happened to one of them."

"Why should anything happen to one of your daughters? Edna, talk to me. Tell me why you're so afraid."

Jordan laid a hand over the liver-spotted claw digging into her arm and tried to draw the widow toward a secluded corner of the open-air restaurant. Planting her high-topped sneakers, Edna resisted.

"No! I can't say anything. I have to protect my daughters."

"I'll protect them."

"That's what he promised. He swore he'd keep them safe."

"Who?"

"I can't talk to you. I can't talk to anyone. Except Bartholomew. I have to find Bartholomew."

Her eyes frantic, she jerked free. Her sneakers made furious squeaking noises as she wove an erratic path toward the door.

Heads turned. The other breakfasters followed her erratic progress with expressions that ranged from surprise to concern to bafflement. Patricia Helms telegraphed a silent question above Davy's head. Duncan Myers was more direct. Frowning,

Bartholomew's financial adviser shoved back his chair and strode across the room.

He was in jogging shorts and a short-sleeved shirt, obviously ready for a run. Unlike Edna's sneakers, his high-dollar Nikes didn't make a sound.

"May I ask what that was about? Mrs. Albert is a very valued guest," he added when Jordan hesitated. "Bartholomew will want to know if one of the staff has said or done something to upset her."

"It wasn't the staff. It was Harry McShay."

"Harry? But he left yesterday." Myers essayed a thin smile. "Surely Mrs. Albert isn't that upset because one of her poker partners deserted her?"

"Apparently Harry did more than simply desert her. Edna just heard Mr. McShay was killed last night."

The smile fell off his face. "Dear God! How?"

"According to Edna, who got it from Felicity, Harry was gunned down at the Oakland airport."

The shock was genuine. The blood drained from Myers's cheeks. His face turned ashen. Now if only Jordan knew whether it stemmed from distress over the loss of a wealthy client or a valuable courier.

"Excuse me. I have to inform Bartholomew about this."

He started for the door, swung back, and made a visible attempt to collect his scattered thoughts.

"Was that all Mrs. Albert said? I thought I heard her mention something about her daughters?"

No way Jordan was confirming anything until

she cornered Edna and found out what had put that terror in her eyes.

"You must have heard wrong."

"I must have." Myers's palmed his shining crown with a shaking hand. "Excuse me."

He hurried out of the restaurant. Jordan followed a moment later. Edna was trying to track down Bartholomew. So was Duncan Myers. She wanted to intercept the widow before Edna bumped into Myers *or* Greene. Cursing the institute's prohibition on cell phones for everyone but staff, she darted around an oleander bush and thumbed her earring.

"Rigger, get TJ Scott on the net. Tell him I need a fix on Bartholomew Greene's current location. Like, fast."

"Stand by, Diamond."

Rigger responded less than a minute later. "Scott says Greene is at his residence. He's just finishing breakfast and is about to depart for the Meditation Center."

"Tell Scott to meet me at the Meditation Center."

Thumbing her earring again, Jordan started down the path that led around the bluffs. The mounded hibiscus bushes to the left passed in a blur of bright red blossoms. The thick, bushy palmetto palms on the right swayed in the wind.

Except it wasn't the breeze causing the fan-shaped leaves to ripple, she discovered when a foot thrust out and tripped her.

Momentum pitched her forward. She threw up

her hands to break her fall, felt her fingers tangle in the thin gold chain that held her emerald, and went down hard. Black, glistening cinders scraped the skin from her right forearm and gouged into her kneecaps.

Then something crashed into the back of her skull and the rest of the world went black as well.

Chapter 15

TJ checked his watch for the third time. A good twenty minutes had passed since Jordan's cryptic message. His impatience was mounting by the second. So was his uneasiness. Wondering what the hell had precipitated Jordan's urgent request for Bartholomew's location, TJ paced the airy, high-ceilinged hall of the Mediation Center.

The door opened. The sound of female voices spun him around. He smothered a curse as Felicity Waller-Winston walked in with an older woman wearing a pink flowered visor and shirt with white tennis shorts. Felicity looked grim, the other guest shocked.

"I heard it on CNN. He was shot in the head."

The older woman clucked in dismay. "How awful for Harry's folks. I remember him saying they'd taken his wife's and daughter's deaths almost as hard as he had. Now this!"

Neither woman noticed TJ until he stepped in front of them. "Felicity, have you seen Jordan?"

"No, I haven't. Did you hear about Harry McShay?"

"Yes."

"It's getting so everyone needs a bodyguard these days." Shuddering delicately, Felicity played with the mirrored sunglasses hooked in the V of TJ's shirt. "Are you sure I can't hire you away from Bartholomew? Whatever he's paying you, I'll double it."

TJ had a few ideas of his own about what this woman needed and they didn't include a bodyguard. A keeper ranked close to the top of the list, right after an industrial-size vibrator. Spotting his employer approaching the center, he disengaged and stepped around the two women to intercept Bartholomew at the door.

Greene wore a troubled expression. That in itself was unusual for the serene, smiling therapist. He was also rubbing his emerald pendant with a quick, almost jerky rhythm. The nervous gesture could be a reaction to the news of his patient's death. Or it could stem from the loss of a designated intermediary and a cool quarter of a million in cash.

"Good morning, Bartholomew."

"What? Oh, good morning, TJ. Have you heard the tragic news?"

"About Harry McShay? Yes."

"Edna Albert caught me just as I was leaving my residence and told me it had been on the news. She was quite distraught, poor woman, as am I."

He fingered his pendant, obviously seeking comfort from the stone.

"There's so much violence in this world, so much negative energy. If only I could reach more people and teach them to look inward for the positive—"

TJ cut him off before he launched into a lengthy discourse. "Have you spoken with Jordan Colby this morning?"

"Jordan? No, I haven't. Why?"

"She had some questions about the iris-recognition system," TJ replied, inventing a cover on the spot. "She's thinking of implementing a similar system for her design studio and asked me to meet her here."

"Jordan has been participating in morning group. Perhaps she's already in the meeting room."

"No, she's not."

"We have a few minutes before the session begins. I'm sure she'll appear shortly." Bartholomew's boyish face folded into sad lines. "Harry's senseless death will test the members of the group. Hopefully, I've given them the right tools to deal with such unexpected, unsettling changes. Excuse me, TJ. I need a few moments to gather myself before I meet with my patients."

He started for one of the private meditation rooms, but turned back to issue a request.

"Would you get a message to Duncan for me? Tell him I'd like to speak to him after group. Harry's death wasn't all that had upset Edna. Evidently there's some problem regarding the payment options for her treatment. I can't imagine what, but promised her I'd look into the matter."

Bright red warning lights were flashing inside TJ's head. Pushing through the front door of the Meditation Center, he unclipped the cell phone clipped to his belt and hit the direct line to his Security Operations Center.

"I need a fix on Jordan Colby. Do you have her on the monitors?"

TJ narrowed his eyes against the dazzling sunlight, waiting impatiently until his on-duty security did a sweep of all twenty-four monitors.

"Negative, Chief."

"Check to see if she scanned in or out of her bungalow in the past half hour."

The wait was longer this time. His heart drumming against his ribs, TJ scanned the postcard-perfect setting. Jordan had to be somewhere among those swaying palms and trickling waterfalls.

"Another negative, Chief."

Dammit! Where the hell was she?

"Run her emerald," he bit out. "See if the stone painted on any of the special filters."

"I show Ms. Colby at the Jade Buddha at 8:46."

Eight forty-six. Just a few minutes before she'd contacted TJ and told him to meet her at the Meditation Center.

"Her emerald doesn't pop up on any screens after that?"

"No, sir."

"Thanks."

TJ slammed the lid on his cell phone. He'd start at the restaurant. Maybe she was still there, huddled in a corner with Edna, away from the cameras.

Crushed-lava rock crunched under his boots as he took the path in long strides. The morning sun beat down and reflected off the glistening black rock in a thousand tiny pinpricks of light.

His mind chasing itself in a vicious circle of unanswered questions, TJ yanked his sunglasses from the V of his shirt. He'd have to purchase a pair of Jordan's, he thought grimly, from her line with high-level UV protection for the tropical sun.

His current pair filtered most of the harmful rays. They also reduced the glitter from the crushed black rock—just enough for TJ to spot the thin gold chain lying beside the path. Only half the broken chain was visible. The other half disappeared under the giant fronds of a palmetto.

He went down on one knee, his gut knotting. Slowly, he raised the spiky leaves and followed the snaking line of gold. Near the end of the chain lay the green teardrop.

But no Jordan. Relief exploded through TJ with

the force of a grenade. He sat back on his heels, almost shaking with the joy of *not* finding her broken or maimed body stuffed inside a leafy-green crypt.

The relief lasted all of five seconds. Then he was on his feet, snatching his cell phone from his belt. Jaw tight, he punched in the phone number to Jordan's controller. Two rings later, a female with a nasal twang answered.

"Beltway Cleaners."

"This is Thomas Jackson Scott. Patch me through."

Another voice responded almost before TJ had finished speaking. This one was slow and resonant and male. "I'm readin' you, Scott. Go ahead."

"I need to contact Diamond."

"Well, now, we don't normally contact field agents except at prearranged times."

Or in extreme emergencies. TJ understood the Standard Operating Procedures. Hell, he lived by them every day. One-way communications shielded undercover operatives from signals that might arrive at awkward moments, like in the middle of a conversation with dopers or mafiosi or the theft ring the agent had infiltrated.

"I know the SOP," he bit out. "I also know you can transmit a silent signal, directing your field agent to check in with Control ASAP. Send it. Now."

"Why?"

There was nothing slow about that bullet. The

single word bounced off a satellite orbiting a hundred miles above the earth with megasonic speed.

"She was supposed to meet me almost half an hour ago and didn't show. I just found a gold chain she was wearing half buried under a bush."

"Stand by."

TJ kept the phone jammed to his ear while he swept the area around the palmetto for signs of a struggle. He spotted no blood spatters, no gouges in the soft earth on either side of the path, no sandals or sunglasses or other personal items. All he had to feed his fear was the shattered gold chain and emerald now clenched in his fist.

"We've signaled her, Scott. She should check in with us shortly. We've also got a GPS lock on her transmitter."

"Where is she?"

"Nine and a half miles from your present location, moving northeast at thirty-eight miles per hour."

Whirling, TJ squinted into the sun. The only road heading northeast from the Tranquility Institute followed the jagged coastline and dead-ended at the small state park at the northern tip of the island. It was a wild, isolated place, sacred to the ancient Hawaiians and dominated by the brooding peak the locals called Ma'aona.

It was TJ's turn to bite out a terse "Stand by."

Putting Jordan's controller on hold, he got his on-duty security officer on the line. It took only a few moments to screen the tapes and verify a rental car had driven through the front gate twenty minutes ago.

"Sure looks like Ms. Colby at the wheel. Her face is angled away from the camera and she's wearing a silk scarf over her hair, but I recognize that glittery butterfly on her sunglasses."

Jordan's signature logo.

TJ stood for a moment, trying to reason this out. He'd already had one taste of the woman's independence. She'd ignored his urgent instructions to the contrary and walked out on a deck with a man who, for all they knew at the time, was a hired gun for the Colombians.

Maybe this was a similar situation. Maybe she'd stumbled onto something and decided to check it out on her own. And maybe not.

TJ went with his instincts. Breaking into a dead run, he clicked back to her controller. "I'm going after her. Keep feeding me that GPS data."

"Roger that. I'll also keep trying to raise her. Over and out."

An annoying little gnat buzzed around Jordan's ear, penetrating her red haze of pain.

Someone was hammering spikes into the back of her head. She was bouncing around like a beach ball, up one moment, slamming down the next. Fiery needles shot up her arms into her shoulder sockets. Yet for some reason all she could focus on was that irritating little buzz.

She attempted to get at it by hunching a shoulder. The gnat didn't go away and, she discovered on a jolt of teeth-grinding agony, her shoulder wouldn't hunch. The pain cut into her with the sharp, clean slice of a scalpel. Her eyelids flew up. Her nostrils flared. With a desperate wheeze, she sucked the stink of exhaust fumes.

Blinking, Jordan stared into inky darkness and gradually made sense of things. The buzz came from her earring. The gold hoop was vibrating and sending low-frequency, inaudible sound waves against her eardrum. The pain came from the fact that someone had taped her ankles together and her wrists behind her before dumping her in the trunk of a car.

A moving car, she amended as another jounce thumped her up, then down. Fire streaked from her arms to her shoulder sockets. She was riding the wave of pain when she realized the jounce had rattled something else, something that went clank in the darkness.

A toolbox? A loose spare tire?

Clamping her jaw against the pain, Jordan wiggled backward. She groped behind her, touched a length of metal, felt it up and down with her fingers. When she made out the object's L-shape, she recognized it instantly as a tire iron.

Her stomach heaved. Acrid bile rose in her throat. She gulped in huge, dry swallows of exhaust-tainted air in a frantic attempt to control the nausea. She managed to conquer her queasiness but couldn't stop her mind from shooting back to a musty, one-car garage.

For a sick moment, she was a bruised, defiant thirteen-year-old trying to escape her drunken stepfather. She could smell the fear, taste the hot fury in her throat as she dodged around the junk he'd been working on.

He'd cut her off. Backed her into a corner. Lashed out with a fist that split the skin just above her left eye. She'd grabbed the closest object and put everything she had into the swing. The crunch of the iron hitting bone had followed her out into the icy night.

She hadn't killed the bastard, she'd learned later. Not for lack of trying, certainly. But something told her she'd better be prepared to take out whoever had dumped her in this trunk.

Working blind, she locked her jaw in savage concentration and felt along the length of the tire iron. If this one was like the one she'd used on her stepfather, the L-shaped tool would have a lug wrench at one end and a sharp wedge at the other for prying off hubcaps.

Her probing fingers found the lug wrench. With a hiss of satisfaction, she reversed the iron. The angle was awkward but she managed to prop the tool against the back of the trunk. The sharp edge she manipulated until it pressed against the tape binding her wrists. Locking her jaw against the pain, she started sawing her arms up and down.

The tape parted after just a minute or two. Jordan drew her wrists forward, fighting the moan that rose in her throat, panting hard and fast. The exhaust fumes almost choked her, but the burning agony in her shoulders slowly subsided.

Reversing the rod again, she angled it downward to get at her ankles. She didn't dare saw all the way through that tape. She'd need the element of surprise when the vehicle stopped. She'd have to keep her arms behind her and her legs looking as though they were still bound when the trunk opened. *If* it opened.

The grim possibility the driver might slow the car, jump out and send it careening off one of the island's high bluffs with her locked inside the trunk sent panic bubbling through Jordan's veins. With a vivid mental image of waves crashing against jagged rocks, she scrunched her body and flipped onto her back. Vehicles manufactured after 2001 were supposed to be equipped with an emergency trunk release.

It had taken the tragic suffocation of six children in one week to focus national attention on the dangers of becoming locked inside a trunk in broiling temperatures. The ensuing study had also compiled data on trunk entrapment as a means of confining victims of carjackings or abductions. The startling results of the study led to legislation mandating internal release mechanisms on new vehicles.

Praying she wasn't locked inside an old clunker, Jordan searched the darkness. Relief oozed like sweat from her pores when she spotted the T-shaped handle hanging from the trunk lid. Constructed from a special phosphorescent material that allowed it to shine in the dark for hours after a brief exposure to ambient light, it glowed like a beacon of hope. One quick pull should spring the trunk lid.

Okay. All right. She could get out if she had to.

Her incipient panic squelched, she groped for the tire iron again and attacked the tape on her ankles. She made the cut at the back and sawed until only a small thread of tape remained intact. She fingered the cut, testing it, and kept sawing until she was confident one good kick would part the remaining strands. Then she curled up in a ball and thumbed the back of her earring.

"This is Diamond," she whispered. "Come in, Control."

TJ's cell phone danced on the dash of the green-and-white-striped Jeep he commandeered. A half second later the phone began to ping.

Maintaining a firm grip on the steering wheel, he fought to flip up the phone lid one-handed. He didn't dare take his eyes from the narrow, twisting road. The right side hugged Ma'aona's steep, densely vegetated slopes. The left dropped off into thin air.

The phone pinged again. With a vicious oath, TJ finally popped the cell phone's lid and shouted over the wind rushing around the Jeep's windshield.

"Scott! Go."

The same voice that had been feeding him GPS coordinates and confirming the movement of the vehicle ahead rapped out what he'd prayed to hear.

"Diamond just contacted us."

The pressure in TJ's chest eased enough for him to drag in a long whistle of air. It was his first full breath since he'd shoved the emerald into his pocket.

"Where is she?"

"In the trunk of the vehicle ahead of you."

"Is she hurt?"

"She took a whack to the back of the head but swears she's fully functional."

Christ! Jordan didn't go down easy and when she did, she didn't stay down long.

"What about weapons? Is she armed?"

"I asked the same question," the stranger on the other end drawled. "She says she's got a tire iron and knows how to use it."

"Tell her I'm— Hang on!"

TJ whipped the Jeep around a hairpin curve, almost screwing the phone into his ear in the process. His heart dropped back into his rib cage about the same time the left wheels connected with the pavement again.

"Tell her I'm ten minutes behind her and closing fast."

"Will do. Over and—"

"Hey! Pal!"

"The code name's Rigger."

"Right." His fist tightened on the cell phone. "I

need you to tell Diamond something else for me, Rigger."

"I'm listening."

"Tell her I love her."

Silence thundered above the shriek of the wind.

"Did you copy that?"

"I did. So did Lightning and everyone else here in the Control Center."

"Screw 'em. Just pass my message to Diamond."

Chapter 16

Jordan had been in more desperate situations but none more bizarre. Here she was, with her knees doubled up to her chin, gripping a tire iron with lethal intent. The back of her skull still throbbed and she had to take shallow breaths to filter out the fumes. Yet the message Rigger had just relayed drove everything else out of her head.

TJ was ten minutes behind.

He was closing fast.

He loved her.

Jordan thought for a moment the carbon monoxide had gotten to her. She was sure of it when she croaked out a hoarse reply.

"Advise Scott that goes both ways."

"Roger, Diamond."

Chuckling, Rigger switched to the alternate net. She could hear him passing her message and smiled in the stuffy darkness, anticipating TJ's reaction. Before Rigger could relay it, the driver hit the brakes.

"Rigger!" she hissed into the stuffy darkness. "We're slowing down."

She waited, her body a coil of tension, while the vehicle made a turn. The going got rougher then. Jordan set her teeth as the car bumped and rattled over what could only be a dirt track.

She could smell the jungle now. The thick, rich scent of dirt and spongy vegetation seeped into the trunk, overpowering even the exhaust fumes. Long moments later, the driver swung the vehicle in a slow, tight circle, backed up and cut the engine.

"We've stopped."

"I see that, Diamond."

"The front door just slammed," she hissed. "You'd better go no-com."

She couldn't take the chance her abductor would hear Rigger's faint transmissions. She'd continue to transmit from this end, though, so she could send Rigger a verbal ID of the bastard.

Thrusting her arms behind her, Jordan locked her fingers on the tire iron. A few seconds later she heard two high-pitched beeps, like those made by a signal from a key chain remote.

The trunk popped open. Sunlight flooded in. Blinded, Jordan squeezed her eyes to slits, until the dancing black spots resolved into the silhouette of a man.

Duncan Myers. Jordan ID'd Bartholomew's financial adviser by the glare bouncing off his bald head even before she took in his jogging shorts and white T-shirt. The automatic gripped in his right hand didn't waver when she propped herself up on one elbow.

"Duncan!" she exclaimed for Rigger's benefit. She didn't have to work too hard to inject outrage and confusion into her voice. "What in the *hell* is going on?"

"You shouldn't have lied to me."

She struggled up another few inches. "When did I lie to you?"

"This morning, when you said I must have heard wrong, that Edna didn't mention her daughters to you."

"I refuse to gossip about an upset, confused woman," Jordan gasped, letting her words spiral into incredulity, "and you knock me unconscious?"

"We both know there's more involved than gossip."

"I don't have a clue what you're talking about!"

She had to spin this out, keep Myers talking, until she could get close enough to take him down. Or until TJ arrived. He was ten minutes behind her. Seven or eight by now.

"You can cut the act," Myers bit out. "I've had my eye on you since the day you arrived. You're a very curious person, Jordan. Too curious. You've asked a lot of questions. And not just of the other guests. Liana Wu told me you pumped her for information about the institute."

"Of course I pumped her. I'm looking at a multimillion-dollar deal. I want all the information I can get about my prospective collaborators."

Myers wasn't buying it. Nor was he moving any closer to the vehicle. Standing well back, he issued a terse order.

"Sit up, swing your legs over the edge of the trunk and hop out."

Jordan made a show of thumping around to gain sufficient leverage. In the process, she slipped the short end of the tire iron inside the stretchy waistband of her shorts. The long end she kept firmly in her grasp as she wiggled upright and swung her feet out of the shallow compartment.

Metal ridges cut into the backs of her legs, but the vehicle was close to the ground. She planted her feet, steadied herself and pushed upright.

The dancing black spots came back. Dizzy from the fumes and pain, Jordan sucked in deep breaths and gave silent thanks the strands of tape still binding her ankles had held. She needed Myers unsuspecting and closer before she could neutralize his weapon with hers.

Stalling for time, she threw a swift glance around the small clearing. Dense undergrowth and trees dripping long, tangled vines shrouded it on three sides. The fourth side was nothing but open air. Swallowing a quick gulp, Jordan saw that Myers had backed the car almost to the edge of what looked like a three-thousand-foot drop.

"Where are we?"

"On the grounds of Ma'aona State Park."

Oh, God! Ma'aona was the sharp peak she could see from her bungalow, the sacred mountain Danny had told her about—the place ancient Hawaiians came to toss *tapu*-breakers onto the rocks below.

"Unfortunately for you," Myers said with a thin smile, "this section of the park is closed to tourists. Nor is this trail on any of the park maps. I found it by accident when I was up here jogging one day. It proved quite convenient for disposing of another person who asked too many questions."

Jordan shot another look at the jungle-covered ravine almost lost in the mists below her. At least now authorities would know where to search for the body of the DEA agent who'd disappeared months ago.

They'd be searching for hers, too, if she didn't watch herself. Her fingers slick with nerves, she slipped the iron rod free of her waistband.

"Dammit, Myers, what's this about?"

"It's about a quarter of a million dollars that was supposed to be deposited into accounts set up under the names of Harry McShay's wife and daughter. It's also about another half million we planned to funnel into blind trusts set up under the names of Edna's four daughters. All my associates at the other end needed was her signature on the paperwork to open the accounts."

Well, that explained why the OMEGA and DEA scrubs of the Tranquility Institute guests had turned up no anomalies. Myers and friends weren't using the guests themselves as couriers or depositors. Instead, they opened accounts in the names of the guests' relatives, living and dead. The relatives wouldn't know the accounts existed. Nor would deposits to those accounts raise red flags because they would come in under the ten-thousand-dollar trigger.

Slick. And disgusting.

Jordan's arms ached from holding them behind her back, but she had to keep Myers talking.

"A half a million dollars, Duncan? To be distributed among a number of fake bank accounts? Something tells me you were skimming off more than just a percentage of the institute's profits."

"How very astute of you."

"Where's the money coming from?"

"From my friend Alejandro."

"You and Garcia are siphoning money from the emerald trade into fake accounts?"

"Don't play the fool! You know very well the emerald trade is a convenient blind for the big drug cartels."

Bingo!

"It's a very simple operation, really."

Jordan managed to keep from sneering. Barely. Here it came. Like so many criminals, this one couldn't keep from bragging about how brilliant he was.

Get this all on tape, Rigger.

"Alejandro contacts me when a drop is ready to be made. We negotiate an exchange rate and he arranges to have the dollars delivered to various bank accounts I've set up around the country. Once the dollars are in the bank, I feed the funds back to Alejandro and his bosses in Colombia by using them to make what looks like legitimate purchases of emeralds."

"With grossly inflated prices," Jordan finished for him, feigning outrage and fear. "Were you going to suck me into your operation, Duncan? Make me an unknowing accomplice?"

"Of course. Alejandro and I had already set the mechanisms in place and negotiated my brokerage fee. As for making you an *unknowing* accomplice…"

A cold, deadly menace came into his eyes.

"I confronted Edna after I saw you two together in the restaurant. She told me you kept asking why she was so afraid. She also said you promised to protect her. How did you plan to do that, Jordan? Who do you work for?"

"Myself. I design eyewear. That's what I do."

Among other things. She knew her cover was solid. If Myers had ferreted out her OMEGA connection, he wouldn't be asking this question.

"Who do *you* work for?" she fired back. "Is Bartholomew behind these fake accounts you've set up?"

Her abductor curled his upper lip. "All Bartholomew cares about are his pretty, green stones. Alejandro and I keep him happy by supplying the emeralds he wants—legally or otherwise. He reciprocates by allowing me to manage his business affairs as I see fit."

"What do you get out of this? Why are you risking prison, or worse?"

"I've got millions waiting for me in those fake accounts, Jordan. Enough to get me off this damn island and set me up for life. I won't let you jeopardize everything I've worked for. You *or* Edna."

"This is crazy! Two women can't just disappear from the institute. How will you explain it?"

"Only you will disappear. Edna, unfortunately, will suffer a stroke brought on by heat exhaustion. She was already feeling the effects of the sun when I assisted her to her bungalow a little while ago."

"Where she's now lying with her mouth, wrists and ankles taped," Jordan said grimly, "waiting for you to come back and finish the job."

"As I said, you're very astute. Now I must ask you to move away from the car."

"So you can shove me over that precipice? I don't think so."

Her desperate bravado wasn't completely feigned. Matters were fast getting to the crunch point.

"I'll shoot you if I have to, although I would prefer you go over the edge without a bullet in you."

"Why? So forensics can't trace it back to you?" She straightened, tensing her calf muscles, calculating the distance. He was still too far, dammit. "What about the DNA you deposited on this masking tape?"

"If anyone ever finds your remains in the ravine below, I'm confident the wild pigs and other creatures rooting around down there will have consumed the tape."

Along with the rest of her carcass. The fact that Myers could paint such a calm verbal picture of animals gnawing on her flesh told Jordan he'd gone over the edge himself. She injected more urgency and a note of panicky pleading.

"They'll find my rental car! They'll know where to look for me."

"They'll find your car on the far side of the island. Naturally I'll run it through a car wash before I abandon it to remove all traces of soil or vegetation that might track back to this locale."

The murdering bastard *was* brilliant. Jordan gave him that much as she spilled out seemingly frantic entreaties. She had to get closer. Just a few yards. That's all she needed.

"Listen to me, Duncan." She hopped toward him, praying the tape would hold. "Please, just listen! You don't need to do this!"

"Unfortunately, I do."

Another hop. Another desperate plea.

"You can set up accounts in my name, Duncan. Move money in and out. I wouldn't say anything. I couldn't! I'd be in as deep as you."

"I might have considered that if you hadn't made that rash promise to 'protect' Edna. Sorry, Jordan, I can't trust you."

He started toward her, circling around for the right angle to shove her over the edge.

Jordan was ready for him. More than ready. Super-high octane pumped through her veins as she gauged the distance to the gun gripped in his white-knuckled fist. She'd have only one chance to connect with the tire iron.

C'mon, you bastard. One more step. Just one more.

"Hey! Myers!"

The bellow erupted from the dense jungle and swung the would-be murderer's head around. His hand jerked. Only an inch or too. Just enough to throw off his aim when Jordan split the tape on her ankles, dodged right and put everything she had into the vicious swing.

Myers's shot went wild. TJ's hit high and to the left. A small, bright flower blossomed in the accountant's white knit shirt a half a heartbeat before metal crunched bone.

The combined force of bullet and tire iron sent Myers staggering toward the precipice. He teetered on the edge, his eyes rolling back in his head.

"Oh, hell!"

Jordan leaped forward, made a wild grab, snagged a fistful of his white knit shirt.

She tried to yank him clear of the edge. She honestly tried. But he was already pitching backward. She could either let loose of his shirt or go over the side with him. A definite no-brainer in Jordan's book.

He didn't make a sound on the way down. Judging by the way his eyes had glazed, she figured he was already unconscious or dead. Just as well. It looked like a bumpy ride to the bottom of that ravine.

The thud of pounding footsteps signaled TJ's imminent arrival. He dragged her away from the edge with one hand and shoved his weapon into an underarm holster with the other.

"You okay?"

"I'm fine."

Aside from aching shoulders, a throbbing skull and the ringing in her ears from the shot Myers had fired from less than a yard away. Not to mention the bruises she'd acquired while bouncing around in the trunk.

TJ saw the bruises, if not the ringing and throbbing. With murder in his eyes, he drew Jordan into his arms.

"Good thing that son of a bitch took a dive."

They stood locked together, knees bumping, heart hammering against heart, while their muscles slowly uncoiled and the tension seeped away like dirty drain water.

"I got most of it," he said, his voice low and rough. "Your controller—Rigger—relayed your transmissions."

"He relayed yours, too."

Which reminded her…

She leaned back in his arms until she could see his face. "I was particularly interested in your last message. The one Rigger passed along just before he went no-com."

Creasing his forehead, TJ played dumb. "Which message was that?"

"I believe Rigger mentioned the word *love*."

"He did?"

"Yes, he did. If you don't mind, I'd like to hear it from the source."

A smile came into his eyes, and Jordan's heart picked up speed again.

"Okay, here it is, right from the horse's mouth. I love you, Red."

She was almost certain he meant it. She was also pretty certain the emotions rolling around inside her chest matched his. But she'd fallen for this man once and he'd walked away from her.

Granted, it was to go undercover. Still, Jordan just wanted a few assurances what he now felt went more than skin deep.

"Are you sure?" she asked, searching his face. "Tight situations like this, the adrenaline starts to pump."

And kept pumping. The syndrome had a name.

Several, in fact. Claire said the medical community termed it postsituational sexual response. Mackenzie called it the post-op hots. Whatever the label, it hit every agent at one time or another.

Some version of it had certainly hit TJ. His smile tipped into a wicked grin. "Trust me on this, Red. I'm definitely pumping right now, but it's more than just adrenaline."

"Okay. If you're sure…"

She slid her arms around his neck and had started to drag his mouth down to hers when an amused drawl rumbled in her ear.

"Control here. You might wanna cut this transmission, Diamond."

"Roger, Control. Over and…" She thumbed her earring, brushing TJ's lips with hers. "Out."

Chapter 17

The taxi ferrying Jordan and TJ from D.C.'s Reagan National Airport cut in and out of the afternoon traffic with careless abandon. A sharp turn onto Constitution Avenue sent Jordan thumping into TJ's shoulder.

He steadied her, grumbling as he did so. "I still don't see what the big rush was. We could have taken a few days to wrap things up in Hawaii and sent that thing back by armed courier."

That "thing" was the Star of the East. The emerald lay cushioned inside a velvet-lined case that was tucked inside another, innocuously labeled box. The package sat squarely on Jordan's lap, where it had rested throughout the long flight to the mainland. She hadn't let it out of her sight since the communiqué from Lightning, directing her to jump on a plane immediately and hand-carry the emerald to D.C. TJ had been instructed to ride shotgun.

Jordan had barely had time to trade her grease-stained shorts and tank top for slacks and her poppy-red, short-sleeved jacket. TJ was still in his khakis and emerald-green Tranquility Institute polo shirt, looking worse for the wear. Dark stubble bristled on his cheeks and chin, matching his irritated scowl.

"Lighten up," Jordan advised. "We'll deliver the package as ordered and wrap up the op at this end."

That's not all they'd do at this end. She'd asked Rigger to book her a suite at the Ritz-Carlton in Crystal City. She had plans for Thomas Jackson Scott that included a juicy steak, a bottle of fine merlot and hot, hungry sex. Not necessarily in that order.

"I had something I wanted to take care of before we left Hawaii." Still grumbling, he dug into his pocket. "Your boss's call didn't give me time to get the chain soldered, so I had to use string."

The emerald dangled from a length of thin brown cord. Swaying with the motion of the taxi, the teardrop caught the sunlight and threw off glinting green sparks.

"Where did you find it?"

"Under a palmetto bush."

"You probably shouldn't have brought the stone with you, TJ. I never paid for it."

"I did. Bartholomew might even have time to

cash the check before he's arraigned on charges of trafficking in stolen merchandise."

He looped the string over her head. The gem dropped into the valley between her breasts, cool at first, then taking on the warmth of her skin.

"I thought we'd have it mounted with diamonds for your engagement ring."

Jordan blinked. She could have sworn the stone just quivered against her flesh. Then TJ's mouth came down on hers and she couldn't separate the stone's movement from the thumping of her heart.

Jordan was wearing more than the emerald on her neck when she mounted the steps of the elegant town house just a block off Massachusetts Avenue.

The whisker burns must have looked as red as they felt. Elizabeth Wells rose from behind the Louis XV desk, her smile widening just a bit as her glance drifted from Jordan's face to a spot just above her collar.

"There you are, dear. Lightning said to escort you right into his office."

The grandmotherly receptionist who regularly fired at the expert level with a variety of small arms turned her smile to TJ.

"You must be Agent Scott." She held out her hand, her eyes twinkling. "We've heard a great deal about you. Please, come right this way. They're waiting for you."

"They who?" Jordan asked.

"Lightning, Cyrene, Rigger and our special guests."

Jordan recognized the two guests immediately. One was bronzed and blond and wearing a burqa over a Chanel suit. The other was dark-haired, gorgeous, and standing with a decidedly proprietary air next to Cyrene.

Nick introduced the sultana of D'han, then made himself and the others known to TJ. Nick and Claire received firm handshakes, Rigger the bruising grip that expressed the entire spectrum of male emotions. In this case it signified gratitude.

"Thanks for talking me up to that park," TJ said. "And for passing my message."

"No problem." The weathered skin beside Rigger's eyes crinkled. "Anytime you want Diamond to know how you feel about her, you just tell me."

"I think I can handle that myself from here on out."

"Looks like you can," Rigger said with a pointed glance in the direction of Jordan's collar.

Feeling a flush of heat above the red silk, she used Nick's letter opener to slit the seal on the box she'd ferried from Hawaii. Withdrawing the inner case, she presented it to the sultana.

"I think this belongs to you."

"Yes," the tall, elegant blonde murmured, raising the lid. "It does indeed."

The egg-shaped emerald outweighed the gem Jordan wore by a good 850 carats. She wouldn't have traded one for the other, though. Somehow the teardrop seemed to have become a permanent part of her energy field.

"I must apologize for requesting that you deliver the Star so quickly," the sultana said. "I'm flying home later this afternoon and very much wished to take it with me. You and Thomas must come for a visit to D'han. Perhaps on your honeymoon, which my darling Nick tells me may take place soon."

When her darling Nick escorted the sultana out a few moments later, Jordan took advantage of the momentary lull to demand an explanation from Luis Esteban.

"I thought you were returning to Colombia after Hong Kong?"

"I did return."

"You didn't stay long."

His silky mustache lifted in a feral smile. "When we arrived in Bogotá, Alejandro heard of the shooting and car explosion at LAX. He let slip some rather incautious remarks that confirmed what I had suspected for some time. He was the pig who lured Maria Fuentes to her death."

"Where's Garcia now?" TJ wanted to know.

"Let us just say Señor Garcia met with an unfortunate accident while visiting the Muzo mine."

The two men's eyes locked. A wolfish grin sketched across TJ's face, a satisfied one across the colonel's.

"You do good work, Esteban."

"As do you, Scott."

"Perhaps we'll work another op together."

"Perhaps we will. And sooner than you think." Esteban's expression turned serious. "While we were waiting for you and Jordan to arrive, I spoke to Lightning about the shipments of unauthorized cargo coming into the United States from my country and others in Central and South America."

"What kind of cargo?"

"Human beings," Claire answered for him. "Undesirables who, for a variety of reasons, have been denied legal entry."

"Is Lightning thinking of mounting an operation?"

"He's considering it."

Esteban's dark eyes rested on Claire. "As you speak Spanish, *querida,* I shall request that we work closely on this mission. Very closely."

Rigger registered an instant protest. "Hold on there, pardner! Diamond and Cyrene went into the field on this op. The next one's mine."

"Do you speak Spanish?"

"I can make myself understood."

"I'm fairly fluent," Jordan volunteered, only to feel the emerald dance against her breasts.

She almost jumped out of her skin. The thing was taking on a life of its own. Belatedly, she realized it was TJ tugging on her string.

"We've got three years of lost time to make up for. Don't make any other plans for the immediate future."

Jordan's belly curled in delight. TJ didn't know it, but their immediate future included a fat rib eye, a couple of glasses of merlot and hot sex.

Definitely not in that order!

* * * * *

ATHENA FORCE

CHOSEN FOR THEIR TALENTS.
TRAINED TO BE THE BEST.
EXPECTED TO CHANGE THE WORLD.

The women of Athena Academy are back.
Don't miss their compelling new adventures
as they reveal the truth about their founder's
unsolved murder—and provoke the wrath of a
cunning new enemy....

FLASHBACK
by Justine DAVIS

Available April 2006 at your favorite retail outlet.

MORE ATHENA ADVENTURES
COMING SOON:

Look-Alike by Meredith Fletcher, May 2006
Exclusive by Katherine Garbera, June 2006
Pawn by Carla Cassidy, July 2006
Comeback by Doranna Durgin, August 2006

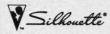

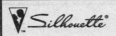